Taken by Two Elves

Twenty-year-old Nicole Glass is thrilled to get hired as an elf at The Naughty Elf Workshop. The extra money will help pay for her upcoming night courses. When she's asked to be a "window elf mannequin" with her two hot male co-workers, the job quickly gets naughty when she's taken by two elves.

I0622939

Taken by Two Elves

Taken

Jasmine Black

Published by Spunky Girl Publishing, 2022.

Copyright

Also by Jasmine Black

Author Note

This is a work of fiction. Characters, places, settings, and events presented in this book are purely of the author's imagination and bear no resemblance to any actual person, living or dead or to any actual events, places, and/or settings.

Chapter One

Wanted *female elves for The Naughty Elf Workshop.*
You will be expected to dress and undress for the occasion. You will impress Santa with naughty chores as well as be a window dressing with other elves and naughty toys. Other duties will be presented after hire.

All sexy elf costumes will be supplied. Eighteen years of age or older only. The pay is high scale, part time and right through the Christmas holidays. Serious applicants only. Please deliver your resume in person to The Naughty Elf Workshop.

No appointment needed. No telephone inquiries please. All questions will be answered in person.

I kept staring at the fancy green and red bordered flyer with bold calligraphy type and a translucent background of two barely dressed male elves kissing an also barely dressed female elf. I had found the flyer tucked in my apartment mailbox.

I'd never been to that shop, but I'd heard rumors through fellow co-workers about what got sold there. Toys for adults and everything was elf themed. I didn't know much about elves except that they were mostly short and dressed in red and green, had pointy ears and pointy shoes.

I was twenty years old, so that covered the eighteen plus part of the flyer. My height would also be a bonus if they were looking for short elves. I was just five foot four inches and that was when I was in heels.

I sure could use the extra money for books for the bookkeeping night courses I'd enrolled in for the New Year.

Part time work be good too as I already had a full-time job, but what were their hours?

Moments later I was on their website. Three in the afternoon until midnight were the store hours. Wow, was that a sign, or was that a sign?

I worked as a housekeeper for a luxurious twenty story hotel in downtown Toronto from six in the morning until two in the afternoon and my hotel job was just a few blocks walk to this naughty elf place. I could go with less sleep for a few weeks and the money would come in handy.

I just needed to find out how much money they paid. I looked at the wall clock in my apartment kitchen. It was three o'clock. If I left now, I'd be at the store within an hour with the bus.

First though, I had to change out of my housekeeper uniform and get into a suitable attire for presenting my resume.

I frowned. But did elves have long blonde hair? I guess I could look it up on the internet, but they could always supply me with a wig, if I got the job.

Yeah, I would skip lunch, get changed and get over there by four.

Excitement grabbed a hold of me. I smiled and headed for my bedroom.

I SWALLOWED AT MY NERVOUSNESS as an hour later I stood outside The Naughty Elf Workshop. It was discreetly located in a back alley, but the window display was beautiful.

The edges of the large ten foot wide, eight-foot-high window flickered with green and red Christmas lights. Sprayed on white snowflakes glittered on the panes. The floor was all white and cottony to represent snow and there were two male elf mannequins on display.

Both mannequins had mid back length luxurious brown hair, big brown eyes and elf ears. They wore green velvet hats with red trim and a white pompom at the end. They had matching green tunics with red buttons and a shiny black belt.

Their heads were turned toward me. One elf was bent over, his hands upon his knees, his behind sticking straight out. The other elf was standing right behind him with what appeared to be a large blue dildo with cute little elves tattooed along the ten-inch shaft. He held the dildo in his hand and it was aimed at the other one's behind.

Both elves were smiling sexily, like they had a naughty secret.

I giggled. This was a cute theme aimed for gay men.

But if I didn't know any better I'd think the two elves were real. I stared at them, but neither of the elves blinked or moved.

Amazing.

How did they make mannequins look so real?

My gaze dropped to the standing elf's huge bulge between his thighs. It pressed boldly against a pair of very tight green and red stripped velvet shorts.

My pussy shuddered with arousal at the erotic sight.

I was twenty years old with very limited sexual experience, but if this male elf mannequin had been real, I would certainly entertain the idea of having sex with him.

I swept my gaze to the bent over elf. From this angle I could see an impressive erection that had my breaths coming faster.

Okay, so whomever had done the window dressing had good taste in well-endowed mannequins. I might be able to work here if I got the job. But first, I wanted to see the inside.

With resume in hand, I nervously stepped into the shop and froze as I gazed around. The entire store was huge and it was decorated like an elf workshop.

Two walls were grey-planked wood panelling containing shelves that held neatly folded colorful costumes. In front of the shelves were carousels containing all kinds of elf costumes. Nearby, male and female elf sex dolls were in various stages of undress with sexy costumes. They'd been posed at a long wood worktable that held different elf-themed sex toys; vibrators with elves tattooed on long shafts, nipple clamps with cute little elves dangling from them, butt plugs with elf faces, jewelry encrusted elfin ears and so much more.

Behind the elf sex doll display a fire flickered in the hearth of a large fieldstone fireplace that was decorated with garland, pretty red and green ornaments, dainty yellow fairy lights and Christmas stockings which were filled with adult toys.

"Come on in. Don't be shy!" a woman cheerfully called out.

Chapter Two

I looked around and realized there were no customers here, but a short lady stood in an open doorway toward the back of the store. She was maybe in her early thirties and looked quite sexy half-dressed in elf lingerie.

Elf ears poked out from a tumble of shoulder-length auburn hair. She wore a glimmering velvet forest green colored push up bra with red lace straps and cute little red bows that followed the valley of her voluptuous breasts. She also wore matching velvet green bikini panties with miniature red bows that were draped along the sides. The panties were attached via red garter belt to long bright red stockings. She even wore red and green stripped elf slippers laced with white faux fur and a gold bell at the upturned pointed tip of each slipper.

Wow. Impressive.

Her red-lipped smile brightened when I held up my resume.

"You're here for the elf job. I can already tell that you'll be perfect. Come, let me see your resume," she said with a wave.

She strolled to behind a glass table that contained the cash register and held out her hand. Her dark chocolate brown-colored eyes sparkled with excitement as I handed her the resume.

I noticed her eyebrows were straight and black. Layers of white, brown and glitter gold eyeshadow along with black eyeliner extended outward from the edge of her eyes toward the end of her eyebrows giving her eyes an upward elf look.

Her makeup looked really cool. I wouldn't mind being dressed up like an elf myself.

As she read my resume her eyes narrowed with seriousness. I got the feeling she must be the owner of this store.

"I can see you've had cashier experience in your past at a grocery store and you currently work at a hotel. I'm assuming your hours there won't cut into here?"

"No problem there. I work weekdays there, mornings and early afternoon. I can be here on weekends and from when you open to midnight during weekdays," I answered.

She nodded and slapped my resume on to the glass countertop making me jump.

"You are petite. Blonde and of age. Are you comfortable showing off intimate parts of your body?" she asked and stared straight at me like I was a bug pinned under a microscope.

I blinked. Had I just heard right? Showing off intimate parts of my body? Oh dear.

"The costumes are sexy and some are quite daring like the one I am wearing. I'll be wanting you at the cash register dressed like an elf, and also assisting customers. I will also ask you to be in intimate positions in the window with the two male elves that are there now.

My eyes widened at the words intimate positions.

"You want me to work with a couple of mannequins?"

"I guess we're doing a good job if you think we're mannequins." came a man's deep voice.

I whirled around and found the two elf mannequins had stepped away from the window area and were now standing by the entrance door.

My face flamed as I realized they were real men and they'd been watching me ogling their packages when I'd been outside checking them out.

Oh, man, how embarrassing.

"No more potential customers out there. So, we'll take an early break time. We're heading next door for coffee. Want some?" The taller of the two elves asked.

He stared at me with his chocolate-colored eyes and my tummy did a nice little flip. I realized he had asked *me* the question. Friendly, wasn't he?

"No thanks." I didn't even know if I had the job yet and despite the place looking really nice and cozy, I'd like to leave and catch the next available bus back home if I didn't get hired.

"How about you, Christine?" he asked the lady who'd inspected my resume.

"Sure thing, the usual," Christine answered.

The two elves left and Christine set her attention back to me.

"Now, you didn't answer my question. Are you comfortable showing off your intimate body parts and being in intimate positions in the window where potential customers can watch? There will even be sex shows involved after ten while you are displayed in the showcase window. I leave it up to the elves at how far they can go. But the farther you go, the better the sales. You'll be getting minimum wage plus a percentage of sales. Just so you know that we notice the sales increase with how far you go with the sex acts. Last year the stores sales went through the roof, and each elf walked off with a cool ten thousand dollars. I expect for everyone to make much more this year. So we're doing similar shows this year, just more daring. No worries about cops. I know the cops on this beat. I've paid them off. We are good there. And I'm best friends with dispatch at the nearby police station, so she'll be able to tip us off if someone calls the cops on us. If that happens, we'd just assume innocent positions."

I couldn't believe what I was hearing. There was sex involved? People watched while we had sex? And cops had been paid off?

Like was she kidding?

At this point I didn't even want to know what she meant by different sexual positions and shows in the window. My mind was reeling about the dollar amount. Ten thousand dollars would alleviate so much pressure while I went to night school next year. I was tired of working for other people and I wanted to learn bookkeeping so I could become self-employed and be my own boss.

My parents had always discouraged my idea of being self-employed saying it was too risky. But working for other people just never sat right with me. I just didn't like to be told what to do. Call me spoiled in that way, but that's just how I was made.

"Do I have the job?" I asked.

A crazy inner happiness bubbled through me as my dream of becoming a self-employed bookkeeper suddenly became *very* real.

"Well, if you can handle sexy costumes and sex acts in public then you're hired. You've got a gorgeous mane of blonde hair; you have a nice smile and you have female parts. I supply you with elf ears, the costumes and makeup. You supply the sex. I think you will do very well here. Welcome aboard. That is, if you want the job."

I couldn't believe it. I suddenly had another job.

A very well-paying job from the looks of it.

Chapter Three

"When do I start?" I asked, feeling euphoric.

"Tomorrow. Say at three sharp. We can discuss what you'll be doing with the other elves. Jake is the expert makeup artist, so he'll be doing your makeup. He's the one who asked you if you wanted coffee. And you can fill out the paperwork tomorrow."

I nodded. My head was spinning. That well-hung elf was doing my makeup. This was going to be very interesting.

"Thank you very much. I look forward to working with all of you," I said and extended my hand.

She reached over the table and we shook.

"Welcome aboard. See you tomorrow."

I turned around and practically floated out the door. Was it possible that I could make so much money? Oh my God, it's insane. Wow.

There must be some hook besides the sex. But I had heard the saying that sex sells, so maybe that was all that was needed to make sales.

I didn't care. I needed the money and I wasn't afraid to get into sexual positions.

The job sounded quite intriguing.

No one would have to know it was me here either. I just wouldn't tell anyone. Besides, makeup would turn me into an elf!

As I exited the store I ran into the other two elves, who held coffees in their hands.

They smiled when they saw me.

"So are you hired?" Jake asked.

"Yes, I start tomorrow," I replied.

"Congratulations. I'm Jake. This here is Randall. We'll enjoy having pretend sex with you, that's for sure," Jake said with a chuckle.

"Likewise," I blurted, feeling my face get really hot, despite the cold December chill in the air.

"See you tomorrow. And sweet dreams," Randall said with a wink and they both stepped into the store.

I swallowed as nervousness began to take hold.

Had he meant my having sweet dreams about them and their big cocks? I'd temporarily forgotten how I'd unashamedly stared at their erections pressing against those tight elf pants while they'd stood in the window watching me.

Oh dear. What was I getting myself into?

I'd just gotten back to my fifth-floor apartment when the phone rang. I didn't want to talk to anyone at the moment so I waited for the answering machine to pick it up.

"Hey, Nicole, it's Brian. Just wanted to see if you want to go to dinner and the movies Saturday night. Call me."

Oh, crap. Brian was a guy I had been dating for like, ever. We hadn't even had sex yet. He acted more like a brother than a guy who was into me. Many times I'd thought about breaking it off with him, but something always made me change my mind. He was comfortable, dependable and the only guy who'd been asking me out.

I realized girls could ask guys out, but I hadn't met one that I really wanted to get to know. Except those two well-hung elf hotties in the window of The Naughty Elf Workshop. Now they looked mature and I'd liked the tingles of excitement that had shimmied through me as I'd studied those big bulges popping against their tight clothing.

Just thinking about Jake and Randall and my new job had me singing as I headed for the shower. I ran the water for a few minutes while I undressed.

Gazing into the full-length mirror that hung on the inside of my bathroom door, I studied my body.

I was petite. A bit on the chubby side, but I had decent sized breasts with pretty pink areoles and nipples. I had a waist, nice wide hips, and my pussy was nude.

My first boyfriend had pretty much only done oral on me, citing *we* wouldn't get pregnant that way. I had enjoyed the orgasms he gave me. I'd done oral on him as well, but he'd also complained about my hair. So I began to shave, realizing that with the hair gone I got a more sensitive impact from a man's mouth. Not that I've been enjoying oral lately.

We'd split up because I'd found him boring. Kind of like Brian was boring.

My thoughts zipped back to what Christine had said. I'd be put into sexual positions and would be doing sex shows with the other elves.

The idea of getting up close and personal with Jake and Randall had my body humming as I stepped into the steamy shower stall. I inhaled as the hot water pummelled the back of my head, soaking my hair. Then I moved forward so the jets of water slammed against my tight neck and shoulder muscles. I moaned in gratitude as the muscles began to loosen.

Cleaning up clients' rooms, changing their sheets, making beds, vacuuming and all the fun stuff that went with being a hotel housekeeper really did a number on my muscles. But the job paid my rent, food and gave me independence from my overbearing parents, who wanted nothing but the best for me. Which meant *their* best for me, not what I wanted for me.

Dad had offered to pay my college tuition but only if I took what he wanted me to take, which had been some sort of computer software engineering course. That was the future, he'd said. Well, sorry to blow your bubble, dad. But the future was already happening now. The course would have been three years. Too long for me to stay living at home.

So, I'd declined and he'd said either college or get a job. So, I'd gotten a job and moved out. I mean, why stay home if I didn't have a good relationship with their dictatorship ways anyways.

I spurt a good heaping of my lavender scented shampoo onto my palm and massaged the liquid into my wet honey blonde hair. My hair was thick, naturally curly and it cascaded near to my mid-back. After lathering up, I rinsed. Then I soaped the rest of me with my vanilla-scented organic soap that I'd bought from a lady who made her own soap and sold it online. I loved the vanilla smell as it mingled with the lavender scent of my hair.

I spent extra time soaping my breasts and my nipples, moaning at the cute way both swelled beneath my tender touches. Then I massaged my soapy palms over my tummy and lower to my abdomen. The closer I got to my pussy, the faster I breathed and the more tense I got.

I eased the slippery soap bar between my spread legs, rubbing it up and down and around my ultra sensitive clitoris, between my labia and around the opening of my vagina. The more I rubbed, the tauter my inner thighs became and the quicker my breaths.

Chapter Four

I slapped the soap bar onto the soap dish, then grabbed the handheld showerhead off its holder, aiming the intense spray at my left nipple until it went taut and achy. Then I took care of my other side, targeting the spray over and around my areola and nipple, watching my nipple harden and bead like a pretty little pink rosebud.

I gasped as pleasure sensations began to course through me. I swiftly pointed the jet of water between my quaking thighs directly at and around my already sensitive clit, moaning as pleasure developed and angled through me.

Hurriedly I aimed the spray of pummelling water at my vaginal opening and then back to my clit again. I came on a moan as rushes of bliss hit me like a tidal wave. I shuddered within the convulsions and moaned as spasms seared into me nice and hot.

I kept the spray angling back and forth between my clit and my vagina, imagining a cock thrusting into me. Imagining Jake or Randall standing here in the shower with me, taking me.

Mmm, yes this was nice. Very nice.

I could go on like this all night long.

Suddenly I couldn't wait until tomorrow afternoon to see what wickedness I could get into at The Naughty Elf Workshop.

By the time I got off work and walked briskly the few blocks toward my new part-time job at The Naughty Elf Workshop, I was a nervous wreck. Christine should have named it The Naughty Elf Sexshop because of all those wicked adult toys she had in that store.

Man, usually I felt pretty confident when starting a new job but I kept having thoughts of what Christine had said about sexual positions and sex shows. Maybe I should have asked her to be more specific before asking her if I had the job?

No, stop freaking out, Nicole. Concentrate on why you need the extra money. You're doing this for your dream. It's easy money and it's worth it.

I took a deep breath, inhaling the cold December air and blew out nice and slow leaving a trail of misty white puffs as they escaped my mouth and nostrils. I walked faster and kept up my breathing exercises. Before I knew it I was standing in front of the store.

I stared at that cute window display expecting to see the two elves from yesterday. Disappointment shot through me. They were not there.

I rolled my eyes. How stupid could I be? Of course they weren't here yet. They were probably inside getting ready.

A sign hung on the door. It said in big bold black letters, Will Return. Beneath it was a little clock with one hand pointing to twelve and the smaller hand to three.

Okay, I would just wait here and grab some much-needed courage before I knocked.

But before I could gather my thoughts, a tap erupted on the glass door. An elf stood on the other side waving to me.

I wasn't quite sure if it was Randall or Jake because he had different makeup on than yesterday. Same lovely elf ears though. He had one long braid that went down his front. He was shirtless, wearing nothing but a green Santa hat, a green bowtie and very tight green briefs that really enhanced his bulge. And boy did the man have muscles. Everywhere. His body had been oiled and his muscles shone brightly beneath the lights.

Suddenly I felt quite warm. Too warm as my gaze wandered over the ridges of muscles.

I heard the click of a lock and then he pulled the door inward.

"Come on in, Nicky. We've had bets on you." It was Jake. I recognized his voice.

I stepped inside the store. Warm air breathed against my face and I inhaled the warm scent of gingerbread.

"Bets?" I asked, feeling confused.

He chuckled.

"I had you down for twenty dollars that you would show up. Randall said you would chicken out and be a no show."

"Oh, well, I guess you just won twenty dollars. The coffee is on you then," I teased.

Jake chuckled. I enjoyed the sound of his laugh. It came from deep in his chest.

"I like your sense of humor," he said.

I slipped off my mitts and tucked them in my coat pocket. Then I began to remove my heavy winter coat and was surprised when he helped. He took my coat and waved for me to follow him. He turned and I got a view of his nice curvy ass, the tight underwear leaving little to my imagination.

"You'll get your own key for the store today. So just let yourself in whenever the store is closed. Coats, boots and clothes all go in the back."

I followed him through the back door where Christine had been standing in yesterday and found myself in another world.

Where the front of the store had been decorated like Santa's workshop, with adult toys on display and gorgeous costumes on racks, this back part of the store was an organized mess. There were several narrow aisles with tons of labelled shelves filled with cardboard boxes. We passed an open door, which was the office.

Then another room which contained costumes, a desk, bright lights with mirrors, tons of makeup and makeup brushes. Then he stopped near a fire escape door where there was a coat rack with a few coats, and boots beneath.

He hung up my coat, and I removed my boots.

He showed me my locker and after I placed my purse inside, he locked it and handed me the key for it. I slipped the key into my jeans back pocket.

"Let's head to the lunchroom," Jake said and we strolled down another isle.

"This place is huge back here," I commented.

"For sure. But we use every inch."

He led me to an open door and then ushered me into the lunchroom. The strong scent of coffee wafted through the air.

I noted there were two long tables and several chairs, a cute kitchenette with fridge, microwave and coffee maker. Christine stood there pouring steaming coffee into a mug. She was dressed differently than yesterday and even more sexy.

She wore a white headband that glittered with white jewels. Long white jewelled earrings dangled from her elf ears. Her face was milky white which illuminated her ultra-pink lips and she wore pink and blue eyeshadow that really brought out the auburn in her eyes and illuminated her dark eyebrows.

Her dress was sheer glitter white that flowed beautifully to her knees. I could easily see her nipples through the dress as she sported no bra or slip underneath. But clearly she wore skimpy panties.

Chapter Five

"Thanks, Jake. Looks like you won the bet," Christine winked at me.

"I did," Jake replied. "Okay gotta find Randall and get at the window before the customers start getting here. See you out front, ladies," Jake said and disappeared.

"Need coffee to warm you up?" Christine asked.

I shook my head. I was already feeling too warm after seeing Jake and too nervous to keep anything down.

"You look amazing," I complimented.

She smiled warmly.

"Thank you. Today, I am an ice elf. I love to keep my customers entertained with a new getup every day."

She placed her coffee on the counter and grabbed some forms and a pen.

"Okay, Nicole, before we get started, have a seat. I just want you to fill in these papers. First of all, there is a questionnaire. This will give me an idea what you're comfortable doing or not doing, okay?"

I took a seat and she placed a long form in front of me.

The first few typewritten questions were already jumping out at me, making my heart race with both excitement and nervousness.

Do you feel comfortable being touched? Do you feel comfortable having a male touch your breasts? Do you feel comfortable doing oral to a male? Having oral done to you by a male? Having oral done to you by a female? Are you comfortable being watched while having sex?

Oh my goodness. These questions were so personal!

I couldn't believe what I was reading!

Are you comfortable with vaginal penetration? Are you comfortable with anal penetration? The questions went on and on.

"The questionnaire is double sided, so more on the back. When you're finished filling it, here is a consent form," Christine said, her voice breaking me from my riveting gaze on the questions. She placed another form onto the table in front of me.

"The consent form is just to confirm that you understand what was asked on the questionnaire."

I nodded.

She produced yet another form.

"And this here is a confidentiality contract that you agree not to discuss what goes on here behind closed doors. Just read it before signing."

Wow, confidentiality. Like whom was I going to tell anyway? This was interesting. Who knew so much paperwork would be involved.

"And I've saved the best for last. This is a form for you to fill out for your pay. At the beginning of each day, I'll let you know how much you made the day before based on a percentage of sales and hourly, so you'll have an idea how much money you're making. You get paid direct deposit at the end of each week on Friday. When you're finished with the questionnaire and the other forms and you still want to stay, leave the papers on my desk in my office. It's the first one you went by when you came into the back room. Then find Jake and he'll put on your makeup. Then see me and I'll get your costume."

"Okay, thanks," I answered.

She must have noticed the nervousness in my voice because she grinned and my nervousness almost disintegrated.

"First day is always overwhelming. I'll get out of your hair and let you fill out all the paperwork. Just take your time. Oh, and if you have any questions, write them down on the extra sheet I've supplied and find me. I'll probably be out front." She pointed to a lined piece of paper at the end of the row of forms laid out on the table.

"Ta, ta, for now," she said.

She grabbed her cup of coffee and briskly left the lunchroom, her beautiful sheer white dress flowing like a glittering cloud behind her.

Wow, my head was really spinning. I felt like I was being bombarded with tons of new shit and that I might be signing my life away.

I picked up the pen and began with the questionnaire, feeling my eyes widen as I ticked off yes to the questions I'd already skimmed.

As I kept reading and checking off the yes boxes, each question seemed to get more intimate than the last one. By the time I was finished answering all the questions, I felt pretty flushed.

Was I really going to do all those things mentioned on the questionnaire? There had even been a sexual position section on the sheet with accompanying small drawings; doggy style position, face to face, cowgirl, chairman, and so many more.

I had no idea there were so many possible sexual positions or so many adult toys to be comfortable with. How would I know if I was comfortable holding a toy or having it suggestively touching my body when I didn't even own an adult toy.

I read over, filled out and signed the other sheets, constantly reminding myself why I was doing this. Although making money to achieve my dream wasn't the only reason anymore. Curiosity was taking hold of me.

I couldn't wait to find out what I would look like as an elf. What gorgeous costumes I'd be wearing. If they were anything like Christine was wearing, I'd feel really sexy for sure. Most of all, I wondered what kind of sexual positions would I be in? And what toys would we be using?

This Naughty Elf store was quite an intriguing place!

I had no questions for Christine, so I grabbed the papers, walked to where I remembered where her office was and left the papers on her desk, then I went in search of Jake.

I didn't have to look hard, because he was just entering the backroom as I left Christine's office.

"Hey, was just coming to look for you. All done?" Jake asked.

"Yes," I replied, feeling a bit awkward as I remembered that naughty questionnaire.

"Good, follow me. Let's get you turned into an elf!"

Chapter Six

I gazed into the makeup mirror lined with brilliant bright lights and could not believe I was looking at myself. Jake had totally transformed me into a gorgeous elf in a manner of minutes and I was speechless.

"You'll be a wood elf today," Jake explained as I stared at the delicate elf ears protruding from my hair at the sides of my head. They felt comfortable and I had no trouble hearing.

He'd applied concealing cream to cover blemishes and had put on makeup in such a way as to make my nose look smaller and my chin a bit longer. My blue eyes sparkled beneath the rosy, brown eyeshadow. My eyebrows glittered from the sienna brown pencil liner that he'd applied. He'd smeared on some sort of concealer to hide the ends of my eyebrows giving me a Spock like look.

He'd also styled my hair, commenting on how luxuriously wavy it was as he'd given me side braids that circled around the back of my head and met in the middle, then dangled down. On my head, I wore a crown of dried flowers, leaves and small pinecones.

I had to admit, I looked incredible.

"What do you think?" Jake asked.

"I can't stop staring at myself," I admitted.

"Well, you are beautiful, so that makes it easier for me to work on you."

He thought I was beautiful? I'd never thought of myself that way.

I blushed.

"Well, it appears no need for blush for you. Come on, let's find Christine so she can get you dressed," Jake took off and I jumped from the chair to follow him.

He certainly did move fast and seemed to know exactly where to find Christine. She was in her office.

"She's done. I'll take care of the store while you get her into gear." And then he was off again.

Christine ushered me to a back room that I hadn't noticed earlier.

"Jake probably told you that you'll be a wood elf today. We decided on a woodsy theme. You'll be in the middle of the two guys but facing Jake with Randall at your back."

I nodded as she swept through an arrangement of clothing hanging on a clothes rack. My breath backed up as she pulled out a glittery green bikini top with a matching very short skirt.

"Here, this is our wood elf costume, and here are your boots and other gear," Christine said as she pulled out a knee-high pair of light brown colored suede boots and also a chestnut brown quiver of arrows along with a green bow.

"You will look smashing, trust me. You can change in one of the change rooms over there and then meet me out front. We'll get you into the window display first. I just hope Jake finds Randall. That son of mine is always trying out the new costumes."

Shock snapped through me.

"Randall is your son?"

Christine nodded. A momentary painful look crossed her face, but then it was gone, replaced by a forced smile.

"Oh yes, I had him when I was fifteen. His father was much older than me. Seduced me and then left me pregnant at fifteen. When he found out, he disappeared and I never saw him again. My parents disowned me when they found out I'd been knocked up. It was a scandal to them. So I was homeless and on the streets for awhile."

I frowned, feeling really bad for her.

"Hey, don't look so down. I got lucky. I found a good shelter for unwed mothers where they took care of me. I had Randall, kept him with me through some rough times. I finished high school, took some business courses, came to work here and just like you I started as a window model and assisting in the store. Then the owners decided to sell and I took out a loan and bought the place. My son and I have been running the store together since he was sixteen."

"That's amazing." I couldn't believe her parents had kicked her out just because some guy had gotten her pregnant. It hadn't even been her fault and what was up with the deadbeat dad? Fucking a girl and then abandoning her. What a selfish asshole he must be.

"My window models always have a piece of my heart. It's why I give a percentage of my sales. The previous owners did that for me, so I am paying it forward."

"I do appreciate it." Boy, she had no idea how much.

"Well, you'll have to work for the sales. Being in the window is not easy. Standing in poses for hours gets quite tiresome. But you get plenty of breaks. Now let's get on your costume. Just use an empty change room and leave your clothing there. The customers are already circling out there. They enjoy the shows at the top of each hour as that's when you all get into a new position. I'll leave your boots and the rest right here."

She handed me the costume and smiled. Her sweet smile totally relaxed me.

"You'll do fine. See you soon," she said and quickly left.

I found the change rooms right behind me, located an empty one then hurriedly removed my shirt and bra and slipped on the bikini top. There was a full-length mirror in here and I gazed at my reflection noticing how the bikini was so small that it barely covered my nipples. It was designed in such a way as to accentuate the valley by having my breasts squeezed together and cupped upward with a push up bra.

I hadn't realized I had such large breasts!

A moment later I'd slipped on the tight skirt, which to my surprise emphasized my wide hips and made my waist look small.

Wow, I really looked...not like me at all.

I was a wood elf now. This was incredible.

No one would recognize me and that gave me pause.

I could actually be as sexually daring as I wanted to be in that display window.

This was going to be so awesome!

Chapter Seven

On my way out of the change room I slipped on my boots. They fit well and gave the illusion I had long legs. I slung the quiver of arrows over my shoulder and grabbed the bow and headed to the front of the store.

There were six customers browsing around and when they saw me enter, they all looked and stared at me. I must be a sight wearing barely anything but I had to remind myself that no one knew who I was and that kind of relaxed me.

From the show window Jake waved me over to him. I noticed the area was now decorated with a couple of gorgeous white Christmas trees that glittered with tiny white fairy lights and puffs of cotton were at our feet signifying snow.

I instantly noted that big bulge between Jake's thighs and I grew incredibly warm. A moment later, I sensed someone standing behind me. I couldn't resist but to turn and take a peek.

Momentary fear zipped through me and I stifled the urge to scream.

An elf dressed in a creepy black cape and tight black top and shorts towered over me. He looked evil.

Long elf ears protruded through his hair. Lengthy brown hair flowed down both sides of his shoulders halfway to his waist. His face had been transformed into a ghoulish greyish brown color. Black and gold shadowed his eyes and his cheeks. His eyes glowed green due to some prosthetic and his lips were an icy black.

"Randall?" I whispered. I sure hoped it was him.

"Dark elf to you, my lovely wood elf," he whispered in a creepy guttural tone.

He held up a long mahogany brown vibrator that looked like a two-inch thick, seven-inch-long tree branch. I couldn't help but shiver as he grinned, showing off black teeth.

"Prepare for anal penetration tonight," he warned, then snickered in a growly manner.

"Alright, Randall, tone it down. You don't want to scare the crap out of her," Jake said with a chuckle. He turned his attention to me.

"Just so you know, the two of us will be a couple in love. We will gaze into each other's eyes for the rest of the night. Every fifteen minutes we get a fifteen-minute break. If you want to walk around in the store and chat with the customers, that always helps increase sales. Or if you need quiet time, or food, then the lunchroom or the coffee shop next door. At every bottom and top of the hour my head will move closer to yours like we are about to kiss. Be prepared for that kiss to happen."

Oh my!

"Randall will be the dark elf. He'll be behind you, stalking you with his large tree vibrator. He'll be aiming it at your buttocks. By the end of the evening, he will be pushing it against your ass, he will lift the skirt and show some of your skin back there to the customers. Christine gave me a heads-up that you're comfortable with pretty much everything."

Oh boy, I had lied like crazy the further down I got on that questionnaire, mainly because I didn't really know how I would react and because I didn't want them to think I was a prude. I also wanted the big bucks.

"So, before the night is done, you'll be topless and Randall and I will be showing you and our audience our cocks. Okay, we've got a great crowd already tonight, let's get this show on the road and make some money."

My mind rocked as Jake stood into position in front of me.

I was going to be topless *and* seeing their cocks?

Oh sweet mercy. Floor swallow me up now!

I could barely listen to Jake's further instructions as to my pose. Then he told me to smile softly and to go still like a mannequin. So I did.

He gazed into my eyes and I stared back at him. He had the most beautiful sparkling brown eyes and he rarely blinked. I was truly impressed and tried to do the same thing. But I found it hard not to move. After awhile my arms and my legs grew a bit tired.

From inside the store I sensed customers were coming over and looking at us. Some stood for quite awhile, studying us. I could hear low murmurs and even some soft chuckles. From the corner of my eyes I noticed movement outside in the alley. People were outside watching, just like I had done yesterday while I'd gazed at Jake and Randall trying to figure out if they were real or mannequins.

The ring of the cash register roared in my ears. I started to count the number of times and reached thirty sales when Randall whispered from behind me.

"Break time."

Already? Thirty sales in fifteen minutes?

Jake winked at me.

"Okay, relax Nicky. You did great. Now let's get moving and keep our limbs from seizing up," Randall suggested.

When Christine saw us step out of the window area, she smiled. She looked very happy and she was busy with a male customer who appeared to be buying a similar outfit to what I was wearing and he was examining a vibrator that looked like the thick branch that Randall had been holding.

"I'm going to help out mom, see you in fifteen," Randall whispered as he passed us and headed over to a cute female customer whose eyes widened when she saw him. Then she laughed, realizing Randall was a dark elf but harmless. She pointed to Jake and I overheard her say that she wanted a similar costume like Jake was wearing for her boyfriend.

"Want to go to the lunchroom?" Jake asked as he stepped up beside me.

I nodded and I followed him into the backroom. Moments later we were in the lunchroom and he was making a pot of coffee.

"Having you here is increasing sales," Jake replied as a few minutes later he set two steaming mugs of coffee onto the table where I sat.

"Really?" I asked, not believing that I had such power.

"Oh, for sure. Let's practice kissing. Kissing passionately in front of the customers will really increase our sales."

Was Jake serious? Surely he was joking that he wanted to kiss?

"But we don't even know each other," I teased, feeling self-conscious.

Especially with him being shirtless and showing off his well muscled shoulders and arms and belly and oh boy, it was getting seriously hot in here.

"Yeah, let's start kissing. It will break the ice and when the time comes later tonight, we've already done it and it won't feel awkward."

I was stunned when he sat down at the table right beside me and leaned forward.

He *really* was serious.

Chapter Eight

My vagina clenched with a longing I never knew I had as his head drew closer. I stared at his hot, seductive looking mouth, then closed my eyes and inhaled, suddenly remembering to breathe.

He smelled nice. Like gingerbread. I'd never cared much for gingerbread, but I sure did care now.

His lips covered mine in a kiss that destroyed my senses. I became instinctual and parted my lips, thrusting my tongue into him. My mind exploded as our tongues twined together and the impact sent shudders of pleasure right up my spine.

I reached up and blindly grabbed at his hard shoulders in an effort to keep myself steady.

He cupped my breasts, holding them captive in his heated palms.

His kiss grew harder, firmer as his mouth slid against mine like a heat seeking missile.

And then suddenly he was breaking away, leaving me gasping and stunned at how I'd just reacted.

"There, that wasn't so bad now, was it?" he purred.

His brown eyes blazed with heat and he drew his hands from my breasts, leaving them feeling plump, heavy and branded. He grabbed his coffee and began drinking as if nothing had just happened.

I shook my head and tried to act sophisticated. Like I was used to having a virtual stranger kiss me unexpectedly all the time.

With trembling fingers I reached out for my coffee cup. I couldn't believe how shaky I felt. Couldn't believe that I'd like to have another kiss from him and so much more. My lips were tingling and my breasts felt so needy. Not to mention my pussy was clenching up a storm.

His scorching gaze was set on me as I took a tentative sip of the hot coffee. It tasted good and smoothed nicely down my parched throat. I needed to make sure he didn't realize how sexually innocent I truly was, so I'd best get his attention off me and change the subject back to work.

Time to ask the question burning in my brain since Jake had mentioned it earlier.

"You said I was going to be going topless. Exactly when is this going to happen and how is this going to work?"

He nodded and gulped down some of his coffee before answering.

"Well, since your questionnaire says you're pretty much comfortable with everything. We may as well just dive into it. In order to keep the interest of the customers who come during our later hours, and to also encourage some of the earlier stragglers to return later, we try to change things up at the top of the hour and the bottom of the hour. In order to go topless, you need to make it slow. Let the straps of your bikini go down lower and lower with each viewing."

"Okay, so like make it seductive," I muttered, watching his succulent mouth, wanting another kiss.

"Exactly. And when you are comfortable doing so, you can also adjust this area," Jake reached out and touched the top part of my bikini. His hand was so hot against my flesh I thought my skin would melt as he slowly peeled a piece of material off one inner side of the bra area and then the other side, revealing more of the valley of my breasts.

"Wow," was all I could say as he held up two pieces of green cloth.

"It's designed that way. In layers. I guess Christine didn't have time to tell you. You can peel strips off until you are topless. It's like a strip tease. You can lift pieces off on the sides too. By eleven o'clock the kids will be home and in bed. That's when the hardcore customers come out. That's when you will bare your breasts and Randall and I will expose our cocks for the customers to see. Sales will go through the roof. "

I swallowed.

"Hardcore?"

Jake nodded and he smiled but the light of the smile didn't quite reach his eyes. I suspected something might have happened and from his next words I knew my instincts were correct.

"The people with the big wallets. Sometimes they harass us but we ignore them as much as we can. That's why the previous girl quit. She decided not to return because of the stalker experience."

Dread filled me.

"A stalker?"

"Oh yeah, the stalking got so bad she had to go into hiding with a bodyguard. Thankfully after awhile they caught the stalker. Turned out to be one of our regular customers. A happy ending for her as she is now engaged to her bodyguard."

Good Lord! Was the money going be worth having a possible stalker on my ass?

I was getting a little bit too spooked at this conversation. Time to change the subject again.

"So Jake, what kind of work do you do? You were really intense into the makeup application and I didn't want to disturb you."

"Actually I am a professional makeup artist and hairstylist," he replied with a proud smile.

"Really."

"Yeah. I work at a few long-term care facilities. The elderly ladies love getting made up by me. Makes them feel and look so much younger. I've established morning hours and certain days at several nursing homes so I am able to work here too. I've been here for about five years. This place is kind of addictive. And the money is pretty good, especially through the holiday season."

I nodded. Okay, if I could just hold on until the holiday season was over, I would have it more than made.

Jake glanced over at a wall clock and his eyes widened with apparent surprise.

"Well, we better head to the makeup room. I need to top off your lips with some fresh lipstick and the bottom of the hour is approaching fast. Make sure you have the bikini straps down a bit more when you go out. Let's get working."

The rest of the evening went pretty fast. I stripped parts of the bikini top off and by eleven o'clock there was just the quiver of arrows on my back and cloth covering my nipples allowing customers to see a luscious valley and to admire the plump side curves of my breasts.

My heart began to pound as just moments before eleven o'clock I stepped into the display area where Randall and Jake waited for me.

That's when Jake told me it was the time for me to go topless and for them to show off their cocks.

Chapter Nine

I was so nervous as the two elves reached into their tight garments, that I felt lightheaded. I stared as they brought out their engorged cocks. Their erections were thick and long, flushed with arousal.

Customers were circling inside the store and outside, their voices raised with excitement as they hoovered around us. I could see them from the corner of my eyes. I steeled myself to remain professional, despite a feverish need flooding me. An insane craving to have both of their cocks sinking into my body.

I blinked in shock at that thought. Slammed down hard on the idea of a ménage with these two men. I was supposed to be working a job, not entertaining ideas of fucking two well-hung elves.

"Your turn," Randall whispered as he stepped behind me. I felt my skirt being pushed aside at the back and that branch-like vibrator slide against my clothed sphincter.

Jake had positioned himself in front of me acting like he did this sort of stuff every day. Which he did and if I wanted my dream of being a self-employed bookkeeper to come true, I'd best remain professional and do what I was getting paid the big bucks to do, which was being a sexy mannequin on display showing off my assets so I could make money.

I brought first one bikini strap and then the other strap down off and my arms and then I pulled on the last strip of material. What was left of the bikini dropped away.

Gasps and whispers zipped through the warm air as my breasts were bared for all to see.

Jake said nothing as he stepped closer and handed me my bow. I clenched my fingers around the bow as his head moved forward; his hot lips stopped inches from my lips. Then he slid his hands upon my bare waist. His palms burned my flesh and my breaths came fast. I felt feverish, horny with all these people watching.

This was insane. I must be crazy. Instead of feeling embarrassed at being partially nude, I was actually aroused!

"Keep your hands to your sides. It gives a spectacular side view of your breasts to customers. Just hold your pose," Jake whispered.

And so I did. My nervousness had mysteriously disappeared, replaced by euphoria. All I had to do was keep reminding myself that no one knew my true identity, so there really was nothing to be embarrassed about.

All around me eyes stared at me. Men commented to each other about my breasts and women spoke in low voices about how juicy and big the men's cocks appeared.

The cash register began ringing again. I heard the door to the store opening and closing many times as people entered. I sensed there was quite a large group of customers inside the store now.

Jake stared at me, a soft smile on his face. His eyes were hard and almost black as he looked at me. He was so still. Just like a freaking mannequin.

It was impressive.

From behind me, I could feel Randall's body heat wafting against me. He had to be very close. My anus was clenching with anticipation as Randall gently pushed the vibrator against my tender ring of muscles and held it there.

Instinctively I pushed back against the adult toy, enjoying the hard feel of it. I hoped Randall didn't notice.

His breaths were coming faster and Jake's breathing was getting louder. Movement from below me captured my attention and I looked down.

My eyes widened as Jake's swollen penis jerked. My pussy squeezed as I imagined him thrusting that gorgeous looking cock deep into my vagina. My nipples felt as if they were growing and hardening. My bared breasts were becoming enlarged and weighty as I noticed Jake's gaze drop and latch onto them.

Awareness was bubbling through me at lightning speed. My body hummed with excitement. My senses were on high alert.

My flesh craved to be stroked by their hands.

I *ached* for penetration.

Oh boy, how was I going to be able to do this for another month?

As the minutes ticked by my body ached for sex. I'd been staring at Jake's cock and I was being so mesmerized by it, I hadn't even noticed that if I glanced sideways ever so slightly I could see Randall's reflection in the mirror quite clearly.

He towered over me from behind in his dark cloak and evil makeup, like a dark elf villain swooping down on two innocent elf lovers who were about to kiss each other. Randall's long thick cock was quite erect and one of his hands grasped my skirt aside while he held the vibrator to my ass with his other hand. The silhouette looked so erotic that I couldn't believe I was one of the models. The sight reinforced my craving for sex with these two men.

"Okay, time for last break of the night," Randall whispered after awhile.

I let out a heavy sigh as he drew the vibrator away and Jake stepped back. Both men quickly shoved their heavy looking cocks back into their shorts and to my surprise Randall assisted in removing the quiver of arrows from my back and then produced a pretty flannel blanket with a cute elf imprint. He held it out to me.

"Here, let's head back to the lunchroom," Randall said.

I nodded jerkily as he wrapped the blanket around my shoulders and then he took the bow out of my clenched hand and placed the items against a near wall.

I was surprised that he was taking a break with Jake and me. All the other breaks he'd helped his mother.

"I'll help out Christine," Jake suddenly said and quickly disappeared into the milling crowd. Several men were standing nearby staring at me as Randall touched my elbow and steered me into the back. He remained silent until we reached the lunchroom.

"Listen, you're a smash hit. The men are in love with you," he said with utter excitement as he reached into the refrigerator and withdrew a large paper lunch bag. He sat down at a table and began withdrawing a couple of sandwiches, pudding cups, and pop.

The last time I'd eaten was lunch just before leaving the hotel after work and I hadn't brought anything for supper thinking I could dash out and get something, but I hadn't been hungry due to nerves.

Quickly I poured a mug of steaming coffee and sat down at a lunch table across from him, feeling drained and very aroused. My pussy pulsed with heat and it felt so swollen with need that I wouldn't be surprised if my arousal juices were staining the material on my outfit.

Chapter Ten

To my surprise Randall pushed one of the plastic wrapped sandwiches and a pudding cup in front of me.

"Here, chow this down. Your growling stomach is driving me crazy," he said and grinned. Even though he was being nice and smiled, his creepy dark elf face and glowing green eyes sent shivers through me.

"Thanks," I replied and reached for the food.

I guess I really was hungry because as I unwrapped the sandwich the tantalizing scent of salmon wafted to my nostrils making my mouth water. A moment later I took a big bite and I couldn't help but moan my appreciation as flavors of mayonnaise, dill, lettuce and salmon exploded against my taste buds.

"This is really delicious," I said after a few more bites.

"My mom makes them. She was nice to make some extra today. She said just in case Nicole is hungry," he replied.

"No way, really?"

He nodded and began eating his sandwich. I noticed his gaze stray toward my chest area and I realized the blanket was hanging open giving him a great view of my breasts. I didn't cover myself. I felt daring and not caring if he was watching me. I'd just had Jake watching them up close and personal plus a bunch of strangers doing the same, so another one looking wouldn't bother me.

I just wish he'd come over and start sucking on my nipples.

I started at that thought and forced myself to finish off the delicious sandwich, then the chocolate pudding and coffee.

"Just wanted to give you a heads up about tomorrow's theme. You're going to be an Elf Queen. Your costume and the tons that will be for sale as soon as we can ticket them in the morning just came in this morning's truck. I've already seen the outfit you'll be wearing. It's quite sexy and leaves little to the imagination. You'll definitely be getting a workout from both Jake and I too with the ménage theme Mom cooked up for us." He raised his eyebrows up and down a few times to insinuate very hot.

Oh sweet. Ménage theme.

I blew out a slow tense breath. Like I was barely holding on with tonight's adventure with the kiss still to come from Jake and now Randall was telling me that tomorrow was going to be even hotter?

"I can also tell you that sales went through the roof today. Mom is very pleased with you. Now I'd better shut up as I've said too much already. Act surprised tomorrow when she tells you."

"Okay, I will." It appeared that actress was in the near future for me here as well.

"And here. Suck on this before Jake's lips meet yours," he slid a wrapped peppermint candy across the table in front of me.

"Thanks. The last thing he needs to taste is salmon pudding on my breath," I muttered as I unwrapped the candy.

My heart began thumping like mad as I popped the candy into my mouth. The mint exploded like wildfire against my taste buds. I inhaled and loved how cool and deep it went into my lungs. Just like fresh crispy air.

I gazed at the clock.

"Time to go," I whispered.

Jake was waiting in the window alcove for Randall and me as we entered the front of the store. There were several customers browsing and all turned to observe as I stepped into position in front of Jake. I watched with heated arousal as both men once again brought their cocks into view for everyone to see.

A murmur of excitement shifted through the air all around me and I handed Randall the blanket he'd given me and once again I exposed my breasts.

"Shall we kiss," Jake whispered as he stepped close to me, his warm palms settling upon my waist. It didn't go unnoticed that he wasn't palming my breasts as he'd done earlier while we'd practiced in the lunchroom. Had he copped a free feel?

My breath halted at the heated arousal in his eyes as his warm lips pressed against mine. I closed my eyes and allowed myself to simply feel the incredible awareness snapping through me.

Slowly, ever so slowly, he moved his lips over mine in sultry featherlike movements. Fire breathed through me as his tongue slid into my mouth and he explored in a teasing way that had my breaths coming fast and hard.

And I was supposed to endure this for fifteen minutes?

This was torture.

Intense need uncoiled deep inside my vagina as the hot outline of Jake's cock touched my pussy. I wanted to push my breasts up against his chest and rub my tender nipples against his hard muscles. I craved to reach down and grasp my hands around his shaft and then bring his pulsing flesh deep inside of me.

I could feel Randall's body heat pummel me as he moved close behind. He lifted my skirt and to my surprise, he pulled aside my underlying panty, revealing an ass cheek for everyone to see.

I gasped into Jake's mouth as the branch-like vibrator pressed against my sphincter muscles. The vibrator was lubed! I felt so hot I swore I was going to self combust and burst into flames. Nothing would be left of me but a bunch of ashes.

The cash register began to ring again and I concentrated on the voices of the customers as they chatted with each other and with Christine. Every once in awhile her sweet laughter would split through the air. I really had to hand it to her with this store. She drew a good crowd and I couldn't wait until tomorrow to see how much money I'd made today. I was also curious to find out exactly what costume I'd be wearing and what naughty postures I'd be in.

But this kiss...this kiss was killing me and no matter how hard I tried to distract my thoughts, I could feel Jake's lips press just a touch harder, almost as if encouraging me to kiss him back. So, I finally did, but I kept myself restrained.

Man, not giving into the aching demand of wanting to just be free to kiss him like crazy was killing me.

Actress. I had to remember I was an actor playing the part. I had to remain under a semblance of self-control because if I lost it in front of the customers and started fucking Jake, I'd get fired. So, I played with him. Teasing his lips, clenching my fists and holding back from grabbing his shaft.

Chapter Eleven

F inally, it was time for us three to break our erotic poses. A quarter to midnight had arrived and it hadn't come soon enough.

Randall was quick to drape the blanket over my shoulders, and he and Jake flanked me as we moved into the crowd and then entered the backroom.

I felt so wound up in still feeling the vibrator pressing against my sphincter, Jake's imprint of his cock against my pussy and the tingles from his hot lips that I could barely sit in the makeup chair as Jake quickly and efficiently removed my elf ears and makeup, showing me which makeup removers, cleansers and moisturizers to use in the future when I would have to remove the makeup myself.

Good heavens, he was so professional, acting so cool. And I, was a raging mess of hormones barely understanding a word he spoke.

"I don't think we've ever had such a large crowd this late at night.," Jake said as Randall plopped himself into the makeup chair beside me.

"I think my mom was literally floating all night," Randall laughed.

He'd taken out those creepy green eyes, removed his elf ears and was busily wiping off his makeup.

Suddenly a normal man emerged with the makeup gone. A sexy normal man with nice, toned muscles. A guy I wouldn't mind fucking.

I couldn't believe how casual both men were acting after just having their cocks exposed for everyone to see. After the three of us being in such an intimate pose.

"There is a shower in back if you need to use it," Jake said as he pronounced me finished.

Only if you both join me, I almost blurted.

But instinctively I knew something would happen between the three of us.

And soon. How could it not?

"I'll shower at home. I gotta catch the bus," I told them.

"Just leave the costume in the change room. We'll take care of it. But grab the key to get into the store. My mom says she left one on her office desk for you," Randall said.

I nodded, awed that Christine would already trust me with a key to get into the store.

"Don't go out the front. Use the emergency exit and go to your right. It takes you directly out to the bus stop. The alleyway back there is well lit and fronts onto several other shops that are also open this late. There's a lot of people walking around this time of night. And there's always a small crowd at the bus stop so you'll be fine," Jake assured.

He'd sat down on the seat in front of the mirror where I'd been sitting and was busily wiping off his makeup.

I nodded thanks, still wondering why they didn't appear shaken by the naughty poses. If I had my way...I'd have *my* way with both of them right here.

"I'll see you guys tomorrow, then," I said.

I tossed them a quick wave, feeling very flustered.

Both men waved goodbye and I quickly strolled to the office and picked up the key. Then I rushed back to the dressing room. After changing I grabbed my stuff from the locker and sailed out the emergency door.

The December air was crisp and cold and snapped against my face shocking me into a sobering reality. I'd just bared my breasts to complete strangers. I'd kissed a complete stranger. Now all I wanted to do was to go home and masturbate in the shower and sleep.

Jake had been right about the alley. It was bright and couples walked hand in hand up and down the alleyway and others were entering the open stores. One was an expensive clothing store, another a pizza place, yet another a convenience store.

I grinned. Tomorrow I would treat myself to pizza for one of my breaks.

He'd also been correct about the bus stop. There was a small quiet crowd milling about and I only had to wait five minutes before the bus arrived. Because there were so few stops due to less people, I was home within half an hour, masturbating in my apartment shower while fantasizing about all that had happened today.

Deep down I knew that masturbating wasn't going to hold me in the long run though. I had pretty good instincts and I had the feeling I'd eventually cave and demand that one or both of my co-workers fuck me during one of those breaks. What they'd done to me with those intimate poses had ignited a naughtiness inside of me. In no time I'd been turned into a woman filled with needs and wants that only a man or two would be able to fully extinguish.

I stepped out of the shower, dried off and slipped naked between my warm flannel sheets. I set the alarm and despite feeling wired, I immediately fell into a deep, dark asleep and awoke to my alarm clock.

I blinked as the shrill ringing sound ripped through my bedroom. I felt as if I'd only been asleep a few minutes, instead of a little over four hours straight. Surprisingly, I didn't feel tired. I was excited as I grabbed a hearty breakfast of eggs, toast and orange juice, packed my lunch and dressed. I was out the door by five thirty and to work by six.

Work at the hotel was the same old grind and I slept through one of my half hour breaks waking up thanks to my little alarm on my watch. The rest of the time I waited anxiously to get out of here so I could get over to The Naughty Elf Workshop. When quitting time came I flew out the door and did a fast-paced walk to the store arriving there quite early at two-thirty.

As I passed the display window where the three of us had been posing intimately yesterday, I stopped dead in my tracks. The cute white Christmas trees and other decorations from yesterday had been taken away, replaced by a new theme. There must have been over a hundred white and gold paper snowflakes, popcorn garland and golden ornaments dangling over an exquisite looking brass single bed draped with sheer white sheets and puffy dark green velvet pillows. Red Christmas bows and ribbons adorned the edges of the window giving the arrangement a cute splash of color.

It was absolutely beautiful. Like a Christmas fairyland or I guess in this case a seductive elf bedroom.

My body tightened with awareness as I stared at the bed. Randall had mentioned a ménage theme today so I had no doubt the luscious bed was for me.

Chapter Twelve

On jittery legs I moved to the front door of the store. It was still locked and so I used the key and let myself in, locking the door behind me. No one was in the storefront so I made my way into the back where I spied Jake and Randall standing in Christine's office. When they saw me approach, they waved for me to come in.

None of them were dressed in their costumes or had their makeup on yet.

Christine looked euphoric though as she stood and came around the desk and extended her hand to me. We shook hands as she explained why she was so happy.

"Congratulations, Nicole. You've broke the sales record of our store on your first day. You've each made $3,500.00 plus your wages for yesterday."

Shock snapped through me as Jake and Randall also shook my hand and congratulated me.

"Are you sure? That's a lot of money in one day," I gasped. Surely there had been some sort of mistake.

Christine chuckled as she went back around her desk and sat down.

"No mistake, sweetie. The costumes you wore along with the branch vibrator all sold out. But customers were quite happy to buy other costumes and adult toys. I had another shipment of adult toys come in this morning. Dinner is on me. It'll be ready in the lunchroom at six fifteen sharp," she said with a smile.

Well, no pizza for me tonight, I guess. I sure wasn't going to turn down a free meal from the boss.

Suddenly she clapped her hands, making me jump.

"Come on everyone, let's get ready. The customers will be here at three, expecting a hot show at three thirty. Nicole, you relax until three, then Jake will bring you up to speed on positions while he gets the makeup on our Elf Queen. Randall, love, would you open the store for me? I need to get into costume and I'm going to order our supper. I'll be out in time for you to get ready. Nicole I've hung your costume in the dressing room."

Jake and Randall nodded and we all left her office.

I headed back to remove my coat and get my stuff into the locker. Then I sat in the lunchroom enjoying a nice hot cup of coffee. I tried to relax, which I couldn't do, of course, since I'd just made a big pile of money in one day, and also due to wondering exactly what naughtiness I would have to endure on that beautiful bed tonight with my two male elves while the customers watched.

MY THOUGHTS WERE SWIRLING as I stared in the full-length mirror at the sexy see-through gold dress I was wearing tonight for the ménage performance. It fit me like a glove, illuminating all my curves, showing off the silhouette of my breasts and nipples and the shadowed blonde hair between my thighs.

Jake had pasted gorgeous golden wire ear cuffs over the top of my ears, making me look like an elf but without the plastic elf ears I'd worn yesterday. The cuffs glistened with green sapphire and ruby red jewels and went perfectly with the sheer dress which flowed off me like gold mist. It had a halter top with plunging neckline, gold twine around my waistline and thigh high splits that showed off my legs as I walked. Not that I would be walking much tonight.

The shoes were gold crystal sandals with gold twines that snaked around my ankles and lower calf. And I also wore a diamond encrusted gold crown with delicate drops of green sapphire and ruby red jewels that matched the ear cuffs.

Jake had curled my hair and let it dangle loose. I looked like an Elf Queen and I felt like a beautiful princess.

Once again the makeup hid my true looks, so I felt daring as I strolled out of the change room and down the hall. As I entered the storefront, customers gasped as I walked past them heading toward the window display area where my bed and the two male elves awaited.

They looked gorgeous tonight, their elf ears intact and makeup made them look just like elves. Their long hair had been pulled back and braided off their forehead and sides, gathered at the back into one long braid.

They each wore a green velvet Santa hat with white faux fur trim and white pompom at the tip. They also wore tight green and red stripped shorts that quite clearly illuminated their assets. The rest of their body remained naked, except for the sculpted muscles that I ached to run my fingers over.

Jake had filled me in on what we'd be doing tonight and I'd been in disbelief ever since. But I didn't regret what I'd checked off on that naughty questionnaire I'd filled out. If this daring ménage display nailed sales, I was all for it. The best part of tonight's show was I'd be working on my back, in the bed.

During makeup, Jake and Randall's chuckles and comments about my being able to catch up on sleep while laying on the bed almost made me tell them I'd never be able to sleep with the two of them posing over me. I'd wanted to tell them I would prefer to have sex with them, but I'd held my tongue, trying to remain professional.

As I walked toward Jake and Randall I glimpsed Christine assisting a male customer. She looked rocking hot as a warrior elf, dressed in green medieval dress with a brown leather corset belt and matching brown leather knee knee-high boots. Elf ears stuck out at the sides of her head and her dark brown hair had been pulled back high to the crown of her head and tied into a ponytail which dangled to her shoulders.

I gazed at the customer she was serving and I suddenly recognized him. I just about froze with shock.

It was my boyfriend, Brian!

Chapter Thirteen

The guy I'd been dating for like ever. The guy I'd never had sex with and as I watched Christine lead him over to the sex dolls, I suddenly understood why. He was more into having sex with dolls than with me. And to make matters worse, he wasn't even paying attention to me like all the customers were doing as I walked toward Jake and Randall.

Damn loser. I'd show him how sexy I could be. That is, if he ever even noticed the window show.

My breaths were coming harsh and fast as I elegantly lay upon the cozy bed, loving the warm feel of the white sheets against my back and the soft green velvet pillow beneath my head. I spread my legs wide as per part of our demonstration.

I tensed as Randall came over me with his body. He positioned himself on all fours; hands and knees on each side of me. His concealed package was about a foot from my lips. His eyes stared straight ahead and suddenly he was as still as a mannequin.

Man, he took his job so freaking seriously.

I blew out a breath as Jake climbed between my spread legs. He lifted my dress and placed it delicately around my waist. I wore no panties as they'd asked, so warm air breathed against my pussy, making it clench. Or maybe it was clenching because Jake's shoulders were pushing against my legs as he lay face down between my thighs?

I wondered what he thought while staring at my pussy. Did he want to fuck me? Did he like what he was seeing?

Have mercy! I should be embarrassed, but I wasn't. I was just as excited as yesterday and I could only imagine how the customers must be reacting watching a mannequin ménage unfolding tonight in The Naughty Elf Workshop.

The three of us went still and held our poses.

I wondered what Brian was doing. Had he seen me? Did he recognize me?

Not possible. I didn't even recognize me with my dark eyebrows and the gorgeous glitter gold eyeshadow embracing my eyes. And the makeup made my nose look thinner and my chin smaller.

Although...might he recognize my blonde hair? Or my eyes if he looked into them?

Oh screw, Brian. I had better things to do.

My heart began to pick up speed as I focused my attention to Randall's concealed shaft. It was large as it pushed against his shorts. And he smelled nice too. Like a delicate scent of nutmeg. I loved nutmeg in my mashed potatoes and I got the feeling I would always associate nutmeg from here on out with Randall and what would transpire throughout the night in the store.

Between my thighs I suddenly felt hot air caress my clit.

I stiffened. Was Jake doing *that* on purpose? Or was he just breathing on me.

Another puff of air. My vagina clenched.

Oh God. That feels so good.

Yet another puff right on my sensitive clit!

Instinctively I tried to clamp my thighs closer together but I met strong resistance from Jake's shoulders. I clenched my fingers into the sheets.

No, don't do this to me, Jake. Not now. Not in front of all these people.

I stifled a moan as more wisps of air billowed.

Suddenly I had the feeling someone other than the customers was staring at me.

At the corner of my eye, I caught Brian studying me from outside the window.

Oh crap. Did Brian recognize me? Why was he watching us so intensely? And then I suddenly realized he wasn't looking at me but at Randall, who was crouched over me.

Oh my goodness! Was he staring at Randall's ass? He didn't even seem to comprehend I existed. It was at that moment I realized that my boring boyfriend might be into guys, not girls. No wonder he treated me more like a sister than a girlfriend. I mean all I got from him was a friendly peck on the cheek. No passionate kissing like I got from Jake yesterday and no heated looks like from Randall.

Why in hell hadn't Brian just told me he wasn't into girls that way. I mean, I'd still be his friend if that were the case. He was a nice guy, just not sexually into me. So, why did he keep asking me out?

It came as a great relief realizing that Brian would remain a friend. It also came as a great relief to me when Brian suddenly walked away, a shopping bag swaying happily in his hand. Probably a male elf sex doll.

Now, I could get back to concentrating on the naughty that Jake was doing between my thighs.

Everything that the two men had outlined to me in the makeup room, as to what would happen tonight on the bed, having my clit stimulated by puffs of air hadn't been mentioned. But doing it on purpose, or not, it was arousing me. I could feel the wetness of my arousal seeping into my vagina and then out of it.

Now I understood why they'd said leave my panties off!

Did Jake notice I was creaming? I hoped he did. I hoped he knew how he was affecting me.

With each gust of air against my clit, the tenser I became. How could I keep still when all I wanted to do was begin gyrating my hips against Jake's face?

Having the two men so close to me like this had my breaths coming fast and loud. I just couldn't help myself. I tried to concentrate on the steady cha ching of the cash register. I tried to figure out ways to distract myself, but it was slowly becoming a lost cause.

Fevered heat was fusing through me.

I was beginning to perspire. I never perspired. At least not like this.

I began to smell Jake's scent too as it wafted past Randall.

Cinnamon.

Oh man, I loved cinnamon. Especially around Christmas time. A sprinkle in my eggnog, a dash in my homemade shortbread cookies or a dusting of it in some warm red wine. Just like Randall's nutmeg scent, I knew I would associate cinnamon with Jake and tonight from here on out.

Finally Randall called it. It was break time.

Jake crawled away from between my legs and Randall climbed off the bed.

I was surprised when both men stretched their hands out to me as I readjusted my dress and swung my legs over the bed. I reached out and grabbed and they easily hoisted me to my feet.

Shock hit me as the customers began to clap.

My legs were so jittery that I could barely walk across the floor, but I nodded my thanks and even shook a couple of men's hands as they praised our show.

Man, I was like on sexual fire as I walked, or maybe stumbled, was a better word, into the back of the store.

Chapter Fourteen

J ake and Randall didn't follow me, thank goodness. I headed back to
the lunchroom. I needed a coffee. Hell, who was I kidding, I needed
an orgasm. Bad.

I couldn't even sit down on a chair, my pussy felt so hot and heavy.
My vagina felt open and needy, craving for a big juicy cock to thrust
into it.

I quietly cursed Jake as I made the coffee. What the hell was he
thinking? Surely he hadn't done it on purpose. I closed my eyes and
tried to steady my breathing. I felt edgy as the coffee brewed in the
machine and the delicious scent whipped through the air.

I poured myself a mug and headed for a window that I hadn't
noticed before. It was toward the back of the lunchroom and looked
out into the alleyway I'd used last night. I unlocked the window and
cranked it open just an inch. Frosty winter air poured against my
steaming face and hot neck and it felt so good to finally get cooled,
even if it was just a little.

I had the feeling I might not be able to go on with this tonight. It
was too intense. I just might die from all this stress from the neediness
coursing through me.

Unless...I snuck into the bathroom and masturbated myself into an
orgasm.

Or I could do it right here...

"Sales are crashing through the roof, Nicole," came Christine's excited voice as she suddenly breezed into the lunchroom like an elf warrior and made a straight line to the coffee machine.

Shit! All thoughts of a quick masturbating session flew out the window.

"Oh, that's lovely," I replied as I quickly shut the window, disappointed to have company.

"You did a wonderful job. The guys are keeping the store running so we can finally talk," she said with a big happy smile.

Oh great. I was horny as hell and the boss wanted to talk. How much worse could things get?

"Come, sit with me, Nicole," she patted the chair beside her.

Reluctantly I did as she asked and sat down, fighting the urge to grind my pussy into the seat of the chair and bring myself off right here in front of her.

She reached out to place her hand over mine and gently squeezed.

"It's not an easy job is it?"

I shook my head. May as well be truthful.

"I know because I did the same. When I was a model, the guys that were hired were so unbelievably hot. I mean, they got me terribly excited, if you know what I mean. Sometimes, well, actually many times, I had to seek relief. Sometimes the guys would give it to me. Sometimes we'd even lose control while on display."

She let the words dangle in the air between us.

Seriously? Was she maybe saying I should lose control while being a mannequin? Cut loose and have sex in front of the customers? Like wasn't she afraid of the cops? Or concerned at how her customers might react?

"Sweetie, I can see you're suffering. If you ever need them to give you relief, you just ask them. They understand what you're going through. I mean they're going through it themselves, right?"

Shock zipped through me.

Just ask them? Was she freaking for real? One of them was her son!

Sure, it was as simple as that? Hey guys, I'm horny, please bring me relief. Um, I don't think so.

"You're looking kind of funny at me. I read your questionnaire, I figured you'd be okay with this ménage? With the live show tonight? In front of the audience."

My head was spinning. Live show? In front of the audience? Why was I suddenly getting the feeling I hadn't been told everything about what was going to happen tonight? And then I remembered Jake and Randall had run out of time and I'd had to rush to get on my costume. They'd said they would fill me in later.

Man! What exactly was going to happen tonight?

I should ask Christine. But I didn't want Jake or Randall to get into trouble for not fully briefing me.

"Oh no, I'm fine. Just the coffee. Gets me wired," I lied.

She looked relieved.

"Oh good, for a minute you looked like you might be horrified. I mean that's why I have the questionnaire, so there are no surprises for my employees. It's rare that someone is comfortable with pretty much anything asked on that questionnaire anyway. I just couldn't believe our luck when you filled out that you were comfortable with pretty much everything we might try!" she gushed.

"I try to be confident about my body. I mean sex is natural," I explained, trying to find an excuse. I sure didn't want her to know I would have said anything to get a second job in order to pay for my night courses.

She nodded and sipped her coffee obviously liking my answer.

"That customer you had. The one who you were showing the sex dolls. Did he get what he wanted?" I asked. I'd been curious ever since I'd seen Brian.

"Darling, you'll have to be more specific. I showed those dolls to at least half a dozen men and women in the fifteen minutes you were on display."

"Oh, he was about my age. Right when I came out."

Christine narrowed her eyes.

"Why do you want to know? Do you know him? If you do, I cannot give out that kind of information."

"Just curious. I found it funny that everyone was looking at me when I came out, except him."

"Oh, I see. Well, he did buy a male sex doll. Said it was a Christmas present for a friend," Christine chuckled.

A friend. Yeah, right.

"So, Nicole. How are you enjoying this job. Are you happy here? I mean, the customers already love you."

Disappointment zipped through me. Sure, all the customers loved me, except Brian. Why did it bother me so much now? Earlier, I'd been relieved thinking he was gay and not into me, but now I felt kind of sad.

"It's different than my other job, that's for sure. And much better pay," I admitted.

"Maybe if sales keep up, you might even consider staying," she replied with a wink.

"Maybe," I answered. I wasn't quite ready to give up on my bookkeeping dream though. But maybe I could do this job and go to school during the day?

Renewed excitement shot through me.

Chapter Fifteen

B ut first I needed to get through tonight. I knew what was coming
over the next few showings and I found myself getting all hot and
bothered again. Yet, I also wondered what Jake and Randall hadn't told
me about this live show Christine had mentioned.

Normally I hated surprises. Tonight was no exception.

The rest of the break zipped by a lightning speed and when
Christine and I entered the front of the store, I was surprised to see
such a large crowd. There was a long lineup of people with packaged
items they wanted to buy and they were cheerfully chatting with each
other. It made me wonder why Christine didn't hire more help to help
send them quickly on their way.

But hey, none of my business.

Jake and Randall were waiting for me at the window area. They
nodded greetings and held out their hands to me like perfect elf
gentlemen as they assisted me onto the cozy bed.

My heart was hammering a mile a minute as I spread my legs again.

Both men pulled their shorts down a couple inches below their
belly button, revealing even more muscles. Several woman came over
to watch, giggling as Randall positioned himself on all fours over my
upper torso, his clothed erection seemed even bigger since the last time.

And Jake moved in between my legs once again, his shoulders
widening my thighs even more and sure enough the bastard started
blowing on my ultra-sensitive clit again!

Within minutes I was once again wrapped in arousal. Every once in a while an involuntary moan would escape my lips and my hands would clench tighter into the sheets. With every moan, Jake would back off the intimate blowing of air onto my clit. Customers were coming over to watch and I slowly closed my eyes so I didn't have to see them. But just knowing they were watching turned me on. How odd was that?

When break time came again, I was once again perspiring. This time I could barely walk without wanting to rub my legs together to climax. I would have gotten myself off too had Jake not followed me into the lunchroom. To my irritation, he was chuckling as he poured both of us some coffee.

I ignored him as I made a bee line to that back window. Once again I cranked it open and loved the fresh air breathing against my hot face, neck and chest. I began contemplating an escape excuse so I could go outside and rub my fevered pussy into a snowbank.

"You're pussy sure is creaming up a storm," Jake said tightly from right behind me.

Son of a bitch. I hadn't even heard him sneak up on me.

"Well, if you'd stop blowing on it, I wouldn't be creaming, now would I?" I snapped without looking at him. But I did catch his elfin reflection in the windowpane. He was smiling. What an irritating man!

"Sorry about that. We should have warned you but we kind of ran out of time earlier. The blowing on your clit is part of the program for tonight. The theme is The Aroused Elf Queen. We need to keep you aroused so when eleven thirty rolls around we can all climax together. Sales will be fantastic. So, yeah, we told you all the things you had to do to us, but we didn't get around to telling you what we would be doing to you. I can tell you now though."

I shook my head. *We can all climax together.*

In front of an audience. Would I be able to do it? Or would I have to act the part? Somehow I got the feeling I wouldn't be acting when the time came. I'd probably be dead by then from the lack of relief!

"No, don't tell me. I want to relax during my break time. I'll do what you told me to do. I'll just trust you to do the rest," I replied.

If I knew what they were going to do to me beyond what was already transpiring, I'd probably freak out from the sexual anticipation.

"Here, coffee," he said.

I turned and accepted the beverage. The mug felt wonderfully warm in my hands and the sizzling steam from the coffee intermingled with the chilly air that blew in the open window. It was a delightful combination.

"Do you do these live Aroused Elf Queen shows often?" I asked after I took several tentative sips of the tantalizing coffee. It was hot and good.

"Every couple of weeks, usually on Friday nights, but with different themes." Jake replied.

Oh for heavens sakes! Every two weeks! They were going to torture me on these nights.

"After we close on nights like these, Christine always goes on a date with the local cop on duty. That keeps the cops off our back."

Concern for Christine rushed through me.

"A date with a cop? Seriously? What if she doesn't like him?"

"Christine can take care of herself. She can sense a bad guy a mile away. You don't need to worry about her. She's pretty street smart."

"But is she comfortable with her son...in what he does with her being in the same room?" I blurted.

"She's too busy to watch, Nicky. And I don't know if you noticed but Randall is always in an area of the window showcase where she can't see. What is done in the display is pretty much Randall's creation job. As long as it increases sales, she's all for it."

Wow. The things she did for her business. She appeared to be a very good businesswoman. I guess she had to be to get those incredible sales.

Jake began talking about himself and filled me in on his background, which I found intriguing. He'd followed in the footsteps of his grandmother and grandfather, who'd been self-employed hairstylists. They'd raised him from when he was six years old after his parents had died of smoke inhalation in a fire that had begun in the attic. The house smoke alarms weren't working in the newly purchased century home. The electrical, it appeared, had never been upgraded.

The fire had engulfed their house on the night he'd been having a sleepover at a cousin's home. His grandmother and grandfather had stepped up and taken care of him. While growing up, he'd hung around his grandparent's salon which was in their basement.

"I really loved the way they interacted with their clients. Most of them were like family by the time my grandparents died. My grandfather had a fatal stroke and my grandmother died two days later of a broken heart. Despite that bad end, it was an amazing ride. I wouldn't change it for the world," he said with a laugh.

I liked the way he laughed. Sincere, cheerful and no regrets. I had the feeling Jake was a good man.

Chapter Sixteen

"And it was natural for me to follow them because that's pretty much all I knew growing up and knowing so many of their clients. I've watched the customers get older. Many have gone into nursing homes. Those are my clients now and I still feel like they are my family. I can't let just anyone do their hair and makeup, right?"

It was my turn to laugh and wholeheartedly agree.

"So, are you ready to head back out? Break is almost over," Jake said as he placed his empty coffee cup on the windowsill beside me.

I blinked in surprise. I'd stood here all this time in front of an open window with frosty air breathing against me. I did feel better though.

If you ever need them to give you relief, you just ask them, is what Christine had suggested earlier.

I blew out a tense breath.

Maybe I would ask one of them. But if I did, would I be able to have a fantastic orgasm in front of the audience when the time came?

I would just have to see what else these two had in store for me tonight, before I decided.

The next several window showings were much of the same, with the only difference being that each time Jake and Randall climbed into bed with me, their tight shorts got pulled lower and lower over their hips. The customers were certainly enjoying the daring display we put on because I could hear their murmurs, gasps, comments and the cash register ring a dinging from the constant sales.

I was thankful when the supper break arrived because I was still on fire and panting for air. My clitoris was pulsing and my vagina was clenching. Even my ass was getting in on the action with my sphincter compressing off and on! And I was having naughty cravings for double penetration!

When Jake, Randall and I entered the lunchroom, we found an arrangement of pizzas, a big bowl of Caesar salad and some soft drinks awaiting us upon one of the tables. The delicious scent of fresh coffee wafted through the air from the coffee machine.

Christine must have a pretty good relationship with the pizza place to have them come in and set up such a nice display for us, because the way that cash register was ringing there was no way she had time to do this.

Somewhere deep within me, past the neediness for sex, I realized I'd gotten the pizza I'd been planning to have tonight after all. But after what I'd been through the past several hours I didn't want pizza or salad, I just wanted sex!

And a nice big fat juicy orgasm.

I blew out a tense breath and headed straight for the back window, opened it, and inhaled the frigid air. Randall and Jake seemed to be paying more attention to devouring the pizza instead of devouring *me* and their low murmurs of appreciation of the food grated on my nerves.

Seriously? How could they eat? Didn't they notice how uptight I was? Or was I taking this too seriously?

"You'd better eat something, Nicole. Things are going to get more intense from here on out," Randall called out from where he sat at one of the lunch tables.

More intense? Was he kidding? I was already past my breaking point thanks to Jake and his freaking breaths on my clit!

From the reflection in the window, I saw Randall shoving a giant piece of pizza into his mouth and nodding at me. I, for some crazy reason, wanted to rip off his elf ears and shove them up his ass!

"At least have some salad. It tastes great. Take some pizza home tonight. Have it for lunch tomorrow," Jake suggested as he strolled up behind me. As he neared me, I could feel his body heat waft off him like little waves of lightning that seared through my sheer dress and teased all my nerve endings.

"Here, I brought you some coffee and a bowl of salad. Eat. You'll need the energy. New positions for all of us when we go back," he said.

New positions?

Oh God, please put me out of my sensual misery.

He placed the coffee on the windowsill and I accepted the bowl of salad. It did look good. Romaine lettuce, croutons, anchovies and like he said it would give me energy.

"Thanks," I whispered.

"No problem," Jake said and then he returned to join Randall at the table.

The two men proceeded to chat about sports and hunting and some jokes that had them hooting and laughing.

I remained at the open window, loving the chilly breeze and to my surprise I enjoyed the flavorful salad and drowned my sexual sorrows in drinking the piping hot coffee.

But all too soon, the break was over.

Back at the show window, I trembled as I gazed at the bed and then beyond it. I was stunned that red velvet curtains had been drawn preventing anyone from seeing the show from outside the store. That was a good thing, especially with sex going on in here tonight.

I watched as Jake lay on his back, face up on the bed. He quickly pulled down his shorts and I gasped as his big cock burst out and thrust straight upward up like a flagpole.

Automatically my pussy and ass both clenched and I licked my lips as I gazed at his possibly ten-inch length and the swollen width, which made me wonder if I would even be able to get his large shaft into my mouth.

From the earlier conversation when I'd first arrived today, I knew that eventually tonight I would get a taste of that juicy looking erection.

My trembling increased as I grew even more enthusiastic.

"For the rest of the night, you'll be in the doggy position on all fours. Your head will be downward over Jake's torso. After every break, your mouth will be closer and closer to his cock. Until you take him into your mouth and do oral on him," Randall explained in a low voice so only I could hear.

"I'll be taking you vaginally later on, but from behind. Okay, onto all fours over Jake," he instructed.

My thoughts were reeling from Randall's words. He was going to fuck me. In front of the customers.

Sweet mercy! What had I signed up for?

My mind spun as I remembered that questionnaire I'd filled out upon getting hired. Sure enough those scenarios had been presented to me on paper and I had said I was comfortable in these positions. I also knew condoms would be used.

And I'd signed the questionnaire. Given it my seal of approval.

I wasn't afraid of doing it. I was just...too damned excited. That was the problem.

Jerkily I climbed over Jake's lower half.

Chapter Seventeen

He was grinning at me.

"Payback is going to be a bitch, isn't it?" he said with a strangled chuckle.

Huh? At the moment all I could think about was taking his penis between my lips and sucking him like he was a juicy steak.

For a moment, I didn't understand what he meant by payback and then it hit me as I got into the doggy position, lifted my ass and lowered my face to within a few inches of Jake's jerking shaft.

I smiled as I pursed my lips ready to start blowing air upon his erection.

Yes, payback is going to be a bitch.

But payback was forgotten as I heard the rip of a condom package. A moment later my dress was pulled up and placed upon my lower back and waist. Warm air caressed my bare ass.

Then my eyes widened as Randall cupped my hanging breasts in his large hot palms and I felt the smooth tip of his cockhead press intimately against my throbbing clitoris.

Damn him!

The air all around me heated as Randall's cockhead ever so gently circled my clit. Upon his impact, I forgot everything. Forgot where I was. *Who* I was. I even overlooked Jake's shaft mere inches from my face.

All I could do was *feel.*

Feel Randall's hot hands cupping my clothed breasts, his fingers plucking on my sensitive nipples, his turgid flesh stalking my clitoris.

I have to remain still, came the words from somewhere deep within the part of my mind that was still working.

Do your job. You'll get your release later on.

But how could I wait?

The hard feel of his smooth cockhead had me quietly moaning as incredible sensations whipped through me. Sensitive nerve endings, already frayed from tonight's activities, zipped into hyper awareness mode making my heart beat faster and my breaths come faster.

My body cried for Randall to start thrusting his cock deep into my quivering vagina. I wanted it so badly, I had to force myself from undulating. I had to break myself from pushing my hips back and having him impale me.

I don't know how I managed to do it, but slowly I pulled myself out of the erotic haze that had captured my senses.

I forced myself to focus on Jake's shaft.

God help me, I had a job to do, but I didn't know how long I could remain professional. This job was going to kill me.

I parted my lips and blew on Jake's cock, just like he had done to my clitoris.

I heard Jake's breath catch.

I smiled inwardly and blew some more. I watched his shaft get thicker and longer.

Customers were watching me and what I was doing. I heard women nervously giggling. Men remained quiet and transfixed as I continued to blow softly.

Suddenly, Jake's cock jerked. Precum appeared at the slit of his cockhead.

Thankfully, Randall had backed off teasing my clit allowing me to refocus on the task at hand.

Maybe Randall was also getting aroused?

Jake's brown eyes were darkening as I puffed directly upon his cockhead. Then I slowly blew up one side of his shaft and another puff down the other side.

I loved that Jake's fingers were clenching tightly into the sheets. Just like my fingers had been doing when he'd been blowing on my clit earlier. Tense muscles jerked at the sides of his jaw.

His expression wasn't of smiles anymore though. It was hard and tight. He was fighting for self-control.

Ha! See how you like it!

I enjoyed tormenting him, but the time passed at an agonizing pace, as every once in awhile Randall's cockhead would begin an erotic rub over my engorged clitoris, making me clench my teeth as arousal coursed through me.

Fifteen minutes later we stepped out of the showcase window area to find the customers clapping and congratulating us on a good show. They truly were thrilled.

Man, how was I going to get through the rest of this evening? I was ready to come just by being so close to Jake's cock and in having Randall touching me so intimately.

Suddenly an idea hit me and I hoped it would work, at least in the short term.

Instead of heading back to the lunchroom for break, I opted to help Christine in the store.

Two reasons as to why.

One, I was being selfish.

I doubted I could handle Randall and Jake acting like they weren't aroused back in the lunchroom. I just knew I couldn't be alone with them. If I did go with them, I was going to slip and beg them to bring me relief. Yeah, I needed to come big time, but now I wanted the customers to watch me climax. For some reason, the idea of being viewed while I was having sex, excited me beyond belief.

The other reason I decided to hang out in the storefront is I didn't think it was fair for Christine to be working so much. Especially because she had a date after work tonight.

Her face lit up like a Christmas tree when I let her know I wanted to assist. She asked me to shadow her, so I did. I stuck to her like glue watching how she acted and where items were kept on the shelves. She even showed me how to use the cash register.

The customers were thrilled in having me assist. Their gazes lowered to my breasts, which due to the sheerness of the dress showed off my curves and my nipples.

So, that's what I did between shows. I helped Christine.

It kept me distracted from the feverish need searing through me. But every time I stepped onto that window display area with Jake and Randall, I was too close to losing my mind and my self control.

With each show, my head lowered closer and closer to Jake's cock. Randall's foreplay against my clit grew more intense. The bastard knew what he was doing. He kept bringing me to the edge of bliss and then backing off.

Now, as the three of us stepped into the showroom for the final show, I was quite ready to be fucked into tomorrow, so to speak.

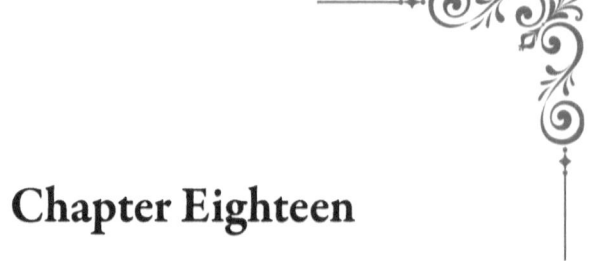

Chapter Eighteen

Even the larger crowd than usual didn't dismay me. Having so many eyes upon me, awed me. Excited me.

I was ready. Hell, I was more than ready.

I was burning up with need as I watched Jake lay down on the bed. He'd sheathed himself with a see-through condom that had imprints of Christmas elves all over it. The condom was cute, and I bet tonight's elfin condom sales would be through the roof, but Jake's big cock held all my attention.

His shaft was engorged, flushed purple with arousal and his brown eyes were so dark that they were black.

I held my breath as I climbed onto the bed and got into the doggy position over his torso and lowered my head close to his penis. Then I let out a slow hot breath right onto his cockhead. His penis jerked.

He swore softly. I smiled.

"Payback was a bitch, wasn't it?" I whispered to him.

"You did great. This part will even be greater," Jake whispered back.

Great? That's what he thought?

Was he for real? I'd been in misery while he'd blown his breath on my clitoris over and over for hours, and when I'd done the same to his shaft, it was great? What the fuck?

Then he smiled and I understood he'd just lied. He was teasing me! The little bastard! I *had* put him through sexual misery.

Good!

But now I needed a fantastic release after all the sexual stress these two naughty elves had put upon me.

Because I was on all fours and I needed my hands to balance myself, Jake would have to wrap his hands around the base of his shaft to prevent his cock from going down my throat when I began bobbing for his pleasure. We'd discussed this technique during our initial get together when I'd gone to the makeup room at three this afternoon.

And now so many hours had passed. I couldn't believe the time to do oral on him had finally arrived.

Slowly I lowered my head and parted my lips.

Gasps came from the onlookers as the thick head of Jake's cock slid into my mouth.

He was *big*.

So thick that my lips were unbelievably stretched to accommodate him. His velvet-encased flesh was so blistering hot that waves of heat whipped off his penis and blasted against my cheeks. His cockhead trembled against my lips as I licked the salty precome from his slit.

I lowered my face some more, allowing a deeper penetration of his penis into my mouth. I kept going until the tip of his shaft touched the back of my throat. I pulled back about an inch and nodded to Jake, indicating this was the safe zone.

He wrapped his fingers around his shaft right where his cock entered my mouth. He would keep his fingers right there, preventing me from bringing him in too deep.

The last thing I wanted to do was gag in front of an audience and ruin the show. Many of them had hung around or had returned for the finale. I noticed their familiar, eager faces and I felt honored. I was going to follow through on this live show and I knew I was going to enjoy this naughty conclusion.

I whimpered as Randall lifted my filmy gold dress over my bare ass and I groaned as his condom-sheathed cockhead slid into my soaked vagina. Then it slipped out and he began a slow massage upon my throbbing clitoris with his wet cockhead.

Oh man, that feels so wonderful.

I could barely focus on what I had to do to Jake as I tightened my lips around his shaft. The silky throbbing feel of him in my mouth encouraged me to continue, despite the arousal coursing through me thanks to Randall and his cockhead teasing my clit.

I hollowed out my cheeks as much as I could to get a better suction. Then I began to bob my head. Up and down I went, bringing his pulsing shaft into my mouth and then out. I went faster and faster feeling his scorching flesh bruise and tingle my lips.

I could hear Jake's breaths coming faster. Could hear his intoxicating moans.

I sure did enjoy the silky throbbing penis as it slid in and out of my mouth. Jake's flesh was so blistering that I was surprised my mouth didn't catch on fire.

I gazed at him and noticed his cheeks were flushed red. His mouth hung open as he panted and thrust his hips upward, pushing his cock heavily into my mouth.

I could feel his penis trembling, jerking. I sensed he could come at any minute.

It appeared Randall suspected it too.

Behind me, Randall began to move.

I moaned with delight as he slid his cock into my vagina, slow and tentative. Maybe he was afraid he would hurt me? He was big too, just like Jake.

Randall's shaft pushed against my clenching vaginal muscles every time he entered me.

I could feel his every thick solid inch as he stretched me. His flesh was hot, like molten lava. I gasped as he withdrew and then thrust into me again, this time deeper.

Oh yes, this feels delicious!

His hands were roasting my flesh as he cupped my breasts and held onto them, using them as a leverage to thrust harder into me.

I could feel the ball of pleasure growing inside of me. Pleasure was ready to explode at any moment. I knew it was going to be good. Really good.

Chapter Nineteen

J ake's shaft was jerking in my mouth and I sensed the time had come for him.

Jake groaned out a warning and that's when Randall thrust so hard into my pussy and so deep that the exquisite ball of pleasure that had been growing inside of me all night, exploded with lightning speed.

I completely forgot about pleasuring Jake as I lost all self-control, undulating and bucking and crying out as the violent shudders wrapped around me and totally destroyed my senses.

Oh dear me! This was good. So damned good.

Randall thrust deeper and deeper into my vagina and I convulsed and moaned around Jake's quivering shaft.

I was flying inside the pleasure. Rolling within the tremors.

Randall stretched into me so beautifully that I thought his shaft would never end. He pistoned so fast and so hard that exquisite colors exploded behind my eyes and I keened at the beauty of it.

The pleasure was spectacular. It was an ecstasy I never even realized existed.

Instantly I knew I was addicted to this. Knew I could never leave here. Not in this lifetime anyway.

I went deep within the pleasure vortex, crying out as the spasms rocked through me like a wild storm of electrical jolts. I bucked and writhed as Randall kept pistoning and kissing me.

The pleasure was insane. It was *that* good.

I don't know how long I stayed within the zone but eventually my orgasm began to subside and I once again became aware of my surroundings.

But surprise washed through me when Jake reached up and gently pushed my head away so that he could withdraw his still erect penis.

I groaned my frustration as Randall withdrew from my pussy and let go of my breasts.

No, I wanted another orgasm!

I moaned out my distress as Randall's hands swept around my waist and he easily lifted me off the bed. A second later, my feet were on the floor and I was standing in front of him.

He grinned and my tummy somersaulted in an enjoyable way.

"Easy baby, we're not finished yet. We're going to make you come again. Lift up your arms," Randall instructed.

More! Fantastic!

Eagerly I did as he asked and brought my arms up. From behind me, Jake lifted my gold dress up and over my head and off my body.

I stood naked between the two well-hung elves and heard the customers murmur with excitement.

Randall's hands held my waist, steadying me.

"Jake's going to take your ass. He'll be heavily lubed and he'll go slow until you relax and accommodate him."

Oh my gosh!

Anal.

I'd experienced anal with a previous boyfriend. Knew it was different than vaginal sex. Knew the anus didn't expand like the vagina and lots of lube would be needed.

When I heard the heavy slurps of lube, my world tilted with excitement. Then came the many slaps of lubricant upon Jake's cock as he prepared himself.

I was trembling as moments later Randall's lips locked onto mine sending my senses reeling.

A second later, Randall's penis slid deep into my willing pussy. My vagina instantly clenched around him, welcoming him back. Then he withdrew and used his cream-soaked cockhead to massage my highly sensitive clitoris.

Immediately the tremors of another orgasm began to form inside of me. It was going to be another fantastic climax. I could just feel it.

Randall thrust into my pussy again and then withdrew.

I cried out as Jake's lubed cockhead pressed against the tight ring of my anal muscles. I forced myself to relax. Thankfully, I hadn't lied on the questionnaire about anal! I knew what to do and what to expect.

As I relaxed, Jake tenderly pushed his hot, thick and heavily lubed penis into my ass. Pleasure and pain intermingled as his cock stretched into me.

I gasped and shuddered, loving the hot feel of his rod.

Slowly he withdrew. I heard more slaps of lube onto his cock and then he thrust into my ass again with excruciating slowness. I loved the burning stretch, enjoyed the thick invasion.

Jake took his time with me and did an incredibly slow pistoning. He stopped every so often to lube his cock some more and then began thrusting the lubricant deeper and deeper into me.

I struggled to breathe as the bites of pain melded with the pleasure. On and on he went, until he was pistoning in an enjoyable rhythm.

Randall kept kissing me, his hot lips feathering over mine with teasing touches and then hard kisses that delighted my senses.

Then Jake withdrew his shaft from my ass and didn't come back in. Randall's cockhead slid into my vagina once again and I knew what was going to happen.

I began to keen with expectation as Randall withdrew and Jake thrust into me. They quickly flew into an erotic tempo.

Jake in. Then out. Randall in. Then out.

Each fiery thrust rocked me toward the pleasure ball that kept growing and growing within me.

And then they both thrust into me at the same time and that's when I lost it.

Pleasure came at me from all directions, drowning me, loving me, killing me.

I convulsed and screamed as I became the filling in an elf sandwich. Their heavy cocks slid into my spasming openings with lightning speed.

Their thick, hot cocks possessed me. Used me. Threw me into oblivion.

My mind exploded and spiralled, all thoughts splintered and were sucked away. My body spasmed and I was carried into pleasure pleasure land.

Their cocks filled me. Made love to me. Gave me so much enjoyment that I kept myself writhing and keening as they slapped their hot muscular bodies against me.

All the waiting, the teasing. All of it had been worth it.

The shudders killed me. The spasms rocked me.

I wanted to stay here for as long as I could. I felt their pistoning get faster, stronger and I knew they were going to join me.

From somewhere far away, I heard their guttural groans and then their shouts echoed through the store.

Oh yes, I was staying here in this job and I would enjoy being taken by two elves every chance I got!

The End

Spunky Girl Publishing Catalog

Jasmine Black
~Erotica~Without the
Romance

Here are some more Jasmine Black stories...

Taken by Two Cowboys

Sierra Allan works hard at her late-father's horse ranch. When her step-brother adds her handy girl services to a private auction to help raise money for the failing ranch, she figures there's no harm...but she's stunned when her services are sold to two sexy cowboys who give her an erotic way to save the ranch—submitting to their dark desires..

Taken by Three Billionaires

Billionaire friends, Liam, Theo and Elijah have just won Princess
Isabella in a billionaire card game. Isabella knows exactly what the
three men will want from her...she just hadn't expected to have all
three of them at once!

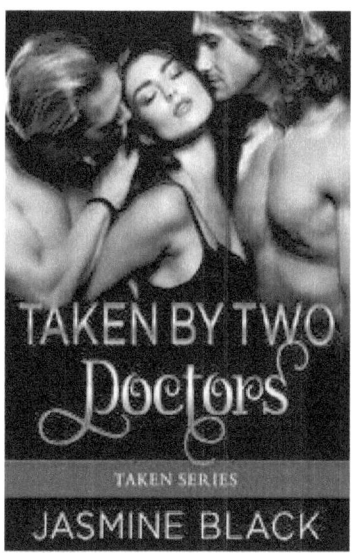

Taken by Two Doctors
A BDSM Medical Fetish Erotica Quickie MFM

Waitress Jean Spelling visits her controversial doctor once a month for some much-needed...stress relief. She looks forward to putting her feet up in the stirrups and enjoys Dr. Ball's naughty unconventional treatments. This time when she arrives, she's surprised to discover that she'll be physically examined by two doctors and they'll prescribe her some much-needed release right there on the examination table!

Stories in Jasmine Black's Ménage series

Stories in Jasmine Black's Taken series

Taken by Two Prison Guards
Taken by Two Elves
Taken by Two Mountain Men
Taken by Two Cops
Taken by Two Santas
Taken by Two Lifeguards
Taken by Two Firefighters
Taken by Two Bikers
Taken by Two Billionaires
Taken by Two Bosses
Taken by Two Cowboys
Taken by Two Personal Trainers
Taken by Two Carpenters

Jasmine Black Website ~ http://www.jasmine-black.com
Twitter ~ @blackerotica1

Jan Springer ~ Erotic Romance ~

Cowboys For Christmas
Cowboys Online 1 ~ Moose Ranch
Jan Springer
A Canadian Contemporary Ménage Romance m/f/m/m Series

Jennifer Jane (JJ) Watson has spent the past ten Christmases in a maximum-security prison.

The last thing she expects is to get early parole, along with a job on a remote Canadian cattle ranch serving Christmas holiday dinners to three of the sexiest cowboys she's ever met!

Rafe, Brady and Dan thought they were getting a couple of male ex-cons to help out around their secluded ranch, but instead they get an attractive and very appealing female.

In the snowbound wilds of Northern Ontario, female companionship is rare.

It's a good thing the three men like to share...

They're dominating, sexy-as-sin and they fill JJ with the hottest ménage fantasies she's ever had. Suddenly she's craving cowboys for Christmas and wishing for something she knows she can never have...a happily ever after.

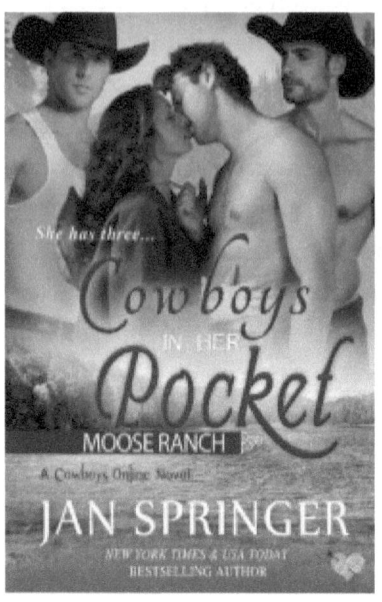

Cowboys In Her Pocket
Cowboys Online 2 ~ Moose Ranch
Jan Springer

After spending ten years in a maximum-security prison Jennifer Jane (JJ) Watson got early parole and a job on a remote Canadian cattle ranch playing housekeeper to three of the sexiest cowboys she's ever met...

Spring has finally arrived at Moose Ranch, and a single woman fresh out of prison shouldn't be experiencing scorching ménages with her three sexy-as-sin cowboys. But JJ's love for her men continues to grow as she gives into the fevered heat and scorching passions she feels for each of them.

Life is perfect.

Until her new life is tested when mysterious happenings occur on the ranch and then one of her cowboys is viciously attacked and injured.

Will JJ's newfound freedom and happiness be ripped away?

Rafe, Brady and Dan never expected to find an attractive and very appealing female to help them out at their secluded ranch. But in the wilds of Northern Ontario, female companionship is rare. It's a good thing the three men like to share...

Brady, Dan and Rafe have never been happier. Their cattle ranch is flourishing and their continued desire to share the sexy woman who cares for them makes their life complete. Until danger threatens to rip everything apart...

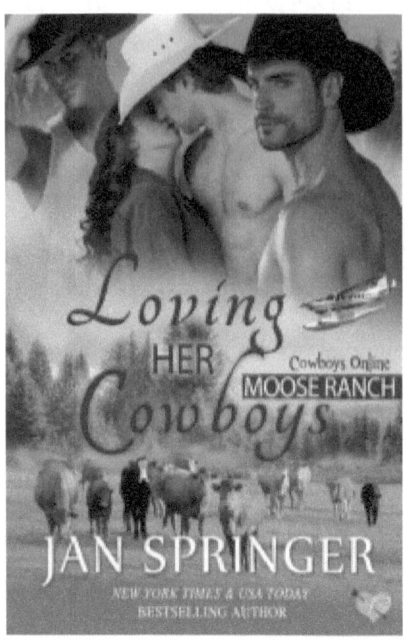

Loving Her Cowboys
Cowboys Online 3 ~ Moose Ranch
Jan Springer

AFTER SPENDING TEN years in a maximum-security prison Jennifer Jane (JJ) Watson got early parole and a job on a remote Canadian cattle ranch playing housekeeper to three of the sexiest cowboys she's ever met...

Her love for her cowboys continues to grow as she gives into fevered heat. But JJ's simmering restlessness explodes and she's seriously making up for lost time by pursuing her dreams. There's only one little problem. She hasn't revealed to her bosses what she's been up to while they're away tending to the cattle. She knows when they discover her secret, there will be hell to pay.

Ranchers Rafe, Dan and Brady have found the woman who completes them. She makes their secluded ranch a home-sweet-home. She's vulnerable, sweet and willing to share her bed with all three of them. But when JJ's secret is unwittingly revealed, they're stunned and angry. They figure it's time to dole out some fiery punishment in some mighty naughty ways...

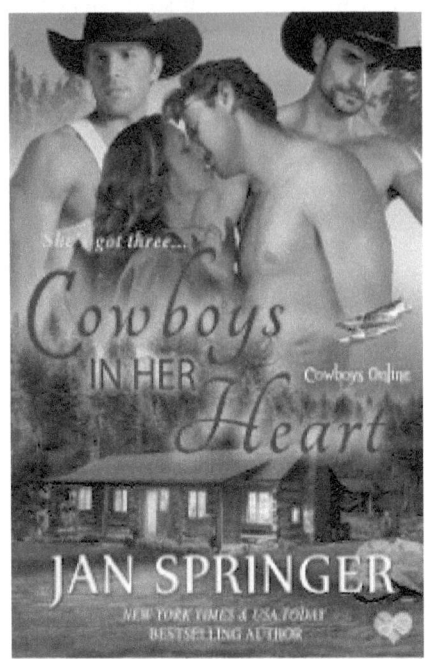

Cowboys In Her Heart
Cowboys Online #4

AFTER SPENDING TEN years in a maximum-security prison, JJ gets unexpected parole and a job on a Canadian ranch serving up scrumptious dinners and lots of hot love to three of the sexiest cowboys she's ever met.

Jennifer Jane "JJ" Watson has never been happier. She's going to have a baby!

Thankfully, their wilderness ranch is a nice distraction for her three sexy cowboys while she's away flying her plane. But when she's home, her dominant hunks are tending to her naughty pregnant cravings and that includes plenty of sizzling ménages.

Rafe, Brady and Dan don't much like the idea of their woman flying the Canadian skies and being at the mercy of the unpredictable Northern Ontario weather. They would prefer having her warming their beds twenty-four seven. But she has a way of getting what she wants and right now she needs her new-found freedom.

Worst fears are realized when JJ, her friend and JJ's plane suddenly go missing and she doesn't come back home to them.

Always Her Cowboys
Cowboys Online 5 ~ Moose Ranch

1

Reader Advisory: Best to read in order. 1. Cowboys for Christmas, 2. Cowboys in Her Pocket, 3. Loving Her Cowboys, 4.Cowboys in Her Heart, 5. Always Her Cowboys. 6. Her Forever Cowboys 7. Claiming Her Cowboys

A Canadian Contemporary Ménage Romance m/f/m/m

JENNIFER JANE (JJ) Watson has spent ten Christmases in a maximum-security prison. The last thing she expected was to get early parole, along with a job on a remote Canadian cattle ranch serving Christmas holiday dinners to three of the sexiest cowboys she's ever met!

Rafe, Brady and Dan thought they were getting male ex-cons to help out around their secluded ranch, but instead they got an attractive and very appealing female. In the snowbound wilds of Northern Ontario, female companionship is rare. It's a good thing the three men like to share...

Christmas is coming once again to Moose Ranch and with JJ's due date approaching, she's distracting herself from anxiety attacks by keeping herself ultra-busy preparing for the arrival of her baby and planning Moose Ranch's first annual Christmas party!

In having a wee baby on the way, there's a lot of stress for Brady, Rafe and Dan. Especially due to JJ's decision on having a wilderness mid-wife deliver the baby *at their secluded ranch* - with *all* of them present for the birth! But their concerns don't stop the men from showing JJ how much they love her...out of bed and in!

With wicked snowstorms, a grounded bush plane, a cheerful holiday party and a sweet baby on the way, the owners of Moose Ranch know this will be one sparkling Christmas season they won't soon forget...

PLUS: HER FOREVER COWBOYS ~ Snowy Creek Ranch #1 Cowboys Online #6

Claiming Her Cowboys ~ Moose Ranch #6 Cowboys Online #7

Risqué Girl Delights Boxed Set
(Contemporary Erotic Romance)

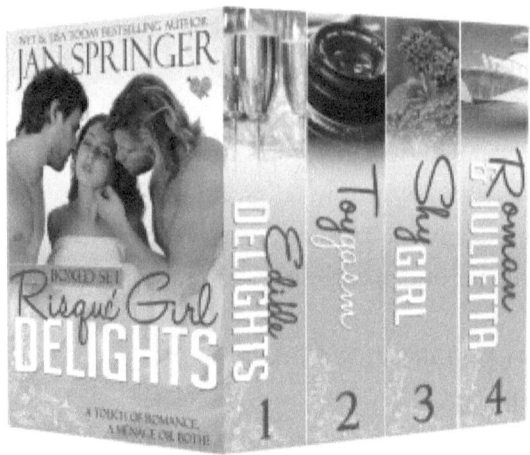

...a touch of romance, a ménage or both?

Edible Delights

YEARS AGO ALLIE MASTERS lost herself in the scorching passion of a ménage a trois relationship with her two bosses. In order to regain her independence, she walked away.

Max and Nick were very fulfilled with their gorgeous assistant. The lovemaking was breathtaking and both men willingly shared the woman they wanted to spend the rest of their lives with. Then she left.

Now Max and Nick have decided it's time to seduce Allie back into their lives.

───── ⁅ঙ৹⁆ ─────

Toygasm

IT'S A CASE OF MISTAKEN identity when the two owners of Sexy Toys, show up for an erotic several day photo shoot of their toys with famous nude model Cammie Creek.

---

2. https://janspringerauthor.files.wordpress.com/2015/02/rgdelights_box_js_3d_noshadow-1.jpg

Cammie believes the two hunks are the male models she's supposed to work with. Usually she doesn't mix business with pleasure, but when they're seducing her right there in front of the camera, she can't resist turning them into her own personal naughty toys.

Josh and Jode are enjoying the perks of being male models; hot lust, sizzling toys and the best pleasure they've ever had. But how will Cammie react when she discovers they're actually her bosses and not just male models?

Shy Girl

FINALLY FREE OF AN abusive relationship, "Shy Girl" Emma McCall sheds her inhibitions and explores her sensual side at Club Rendezvous, a club specializing in the Alternate Lifestyle.

At the club she's surprised to find Logan Masters, a sexy hunk she's secretly fantasized about since college. With Logan's help, Emma will experience her ultimate fantasy - a scorching ménage a trois.

Roman and Julietta

HER PERFECT LOVER...

Modern day pirate Julietta Black's life has always been immersed in the violent and traditional ways of piracy. When her family's arch enemy puts a hit out on her family, Julietta knows there's only one way to lift the hit; she must kidnap the enemy's sexy grandson and force a union between the two warring families. Night after night, wrapped in Roman's strong arms, she can't deny the searing attraction blazing between them. Nor can she deny he now holds her heart as well as her life in his hands.

His dream angel...

When Roman Prince's mysterious captor offers him a luscious woman to bed, fierce desire ignites, melting his usually tight self-control. Lust quickly turns to love as he enjoys their naughty trysts more than he should. How will he react when he discovers he's been kidnapped, not for a ransom, but captured for his sperm?

Alpha Outlaws Boxed Set (Books 1-5 Outlaw Lovers)
5 Books!!

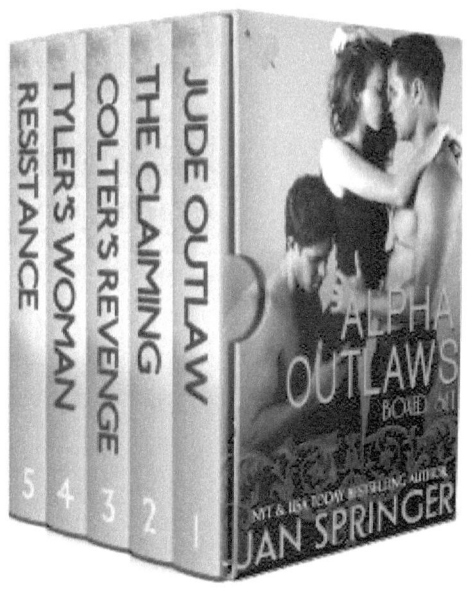

3

IN A WORLD GONE MAD...

A fast-acting virus has killed a majority of the world's female population. With the creation of The Claiming Law, groups of men suddenly have the right to claim a female as their sensual property and the sexy Outlaw brothers are going to declare ownership of the women they love...any way they can.

Jude Outlaw

When Cate Callahan learns Jude is coming home from the Terrorist Wars and is ready to claim her under the new law—with the help of his four brothers—she steals their boat and escapes to the high seas. Unfortunately, her runaway bid for freedom doesn't last long.

Quickly capturing his lover, Jude rekindles the flames and seduces Cate back into his bed.

---

3. https://janspringerauthor.files.wordpress.com/2010/07/alphaoutlaws_js_box_final.jpg

But Jude holds a secret that could make him lose Cate forever...
PLUS

The Claiming

Seeking refuge from the Claiming Law, Callie Callahan hides in a deserted cabin in the Maine woods and is shocked when her ex-flame finds her. She's always craved being in Luke Outlaw's arms. Tasting him. Touching him. Taking him deeply within her. So, what's a girl to do but to delve into the sinful delights he offers.

Luke has finally reunited with the love of his life. He knows there is only one way to keep Callie safe and with him forever. He'll do it with the help of his three brothers and an assortment of naughty toys. Rekindling the flames between them, he unleashes Callie's sensual side, taking her in ways she never dreamed possible, all with the ultimate goal of introducing her to the Outlaw Lovers and The Claiming.

Colter's Revenge

Revenge belongs to Dr. Colter Outlaw when he unexpectedly reunites with the beautiful woman who broke his heart during the Terrorist Wars. Capturing her, collaring her and holding her against her will, he seduces her, fills her with wicked desires and naughty cravings for a delicious ménage. Fully intent on breaking her heart and walking away, Colter's plans unravel when he submits to the carnal pleasures Ashley gives him so freely.

Colter had told her he loved her. He'd whispered promises of rescue from her life as a slave, but when he'd suddenly disappeared, she'd been devastated. Infected with a version of the X-virus that leaves Ashley Blakely sexually excited on a daily basis, she has come to Pleasure Palace to bid on a cure for her illness. She never expected her Outlaw Lover to be there and screw her plans. Nor did she expect to give him her heart and body so easily...

Tyler's Woman

For years Tyler Outlaw and his best friend, Hunter Brown, endured brutal torture and worse in an overseas terrorist prison. Finally, free of their hell, they return home intent on seducing Laurie into their erotic-filled fantasies.

Laurie Callahan has always experienced red-hot pleasure and passionate love in Tyler Outlaw's arms. But when he's pronounced MIA, presumed dead in the Terrorist Wars, Laurie's world is shattered, and her heart is broken.

Shocked to discover Tyler is alive and he's taken a male lover, Laurie is thrust into a sensual world of sizzling seductions, scorching ménages and the carnal desires that both scarred men crave. But she fears Tyler won't want her when he discovers she's not the same woman he left behind...

****READER CAUTION IS ADVISED (m/m forced scenes) ****

Resistance

In the near future, a virus has been unleashed, killing a majority of the world's female population, forcing the introduction of the Claiming Law. A law that states men have all the rights and women are sexual property claimable by groups of men.

Fugitive female...

Renegade Resistance leader Reena "Red" Wilde is in for the fight of her life when she experiences an erotic attraction to the two most dangerous men she's ever met.

Black ops assassin...

Months ago, Will "Blade" Smith spent one sizzling evening in the arms of a red-haired seductress. Now she's his next assignment. One look into her gorgeous eyes and he's wrestling his heated cravings for her all over again.

Bounty Hunter...

When Cade Outlaw nabs his bounty, sexy-as-sin Reena Wilde, his profession dictates she's hands-off. But he can't ignore the magnetic sparks between them...or that she is the biggest temptation of his life.

Resistance is futile...

After Reena escapes Cade and Will and falls prey to a band of evil hunters, she's grateful her sexy hunks come to her rescue...and in return, saves their lives. Trapped in a solitary cabin during a wicked snowstorm, she can't resist her two, well-hung studs, nor can she deny they've claimed her heart.

Many more Jasmine Black and Jan Springer electronic books, print books, audiobooks plus translated stories and print books can be found at http://www.janspringer.com and http://www.jasmine-black.com

Here are ways we can connect:

Jasmine Black Website at http://janspringerauthor.wordpress.com/jasmine-black/

Jan Springer Website at http://www.janspringer.com[1]

Instagram – http://www.instagram.com/janspringerauthor

Facebook - https://www.facebook.com/janspringereroticromance

Twitter Jan Springer- https://twitter.com/janspringer @janspringer

Twitter Jasmine Black - https://twitter.com/blackerotica1 @blackerotica1

Pinterest - http://www.pinterest.com/janspringer1/

Jan's Blog - http://janspringerauthor.wordpress.com/blog-2/

Happy Reading,

Jasmine Black / Jan Springer

1. http://www.janspringer.com/

Don't miss out!

Visit the website below and you can sign up to receive emails whenever Jasmine Black publishes a new book. There's no charge and no obligation.

https://books2read.com/r/B-A-GIJD-HBMDC

Connecting independent readers to independent writers.

www.ingramcontent.com/pod-product-compliance
Lightning Source LLC
Chambersburg PA
CBHW022040170626
46808CB00003B/1287